P9-CQD-579

Cape Diablo shimmered on the horizon, a lush emerald-green gilded by the dying light. For a moment, as the sun hung suspended in a painted sky, the island seemed bathed in gold. A glowing sanctuary that beckoned to the weary traveler.

As they approached the island, the sky deepened and the water turned dark, as if a giant shadow had crept over the whole area. It was a strange phenomenon, a trick of the light that seemed too much like an omen.

Carrie couldn't seem to shake off a gnawing fear. The place seemed so wild and primitive. As the boat drifted silently toward the pier, she became aware of a dozen sounds. Water lapping at the hull…the startled flight of an egret…an insect buzzing near her ear.

And, in the distance, a scream.

AMANDA STEVENS

SECRETS OF HIS OWN

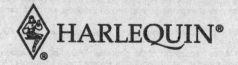

TORONTO • NEW YORK • LONDON
AMSTERDAM • PARIS • SYDNEY • HAMBURG
STOCKHOLM • ATHENS • TOKYO • MILAN • MADRID
PRAGUE • WARSAW • BUDAPEST • AUCKLAND

If you purchased this book without a cover you should be aware
that this book is stolen property. It was reported as "unsold and
destroyed" to the publisher, and neither the author nor the
publisher has received any payment for this "stripped book."

ISBN-13: 978-0-373-88704-0
ISBN-10:   0-373-88704-3

SECRETS OF HIS OWN

Copyright: © 2006 by Marilyn Medlock Amann

All rights reserved. Except for use in any review, the reproduction or
utilization of this work in whole or in part in any form by any electronic,
mechanical or other means, now known or hereafter invented, including
xerography, photocopying and recording, or in any information storage
or retrieval system, is forbidden without the written permission of the
publisher, Harlequin Enterprises Limited, 225 Duncan Mill Road,
Don Mills, Ontario, Canada M3B 3K9.

All characters in this book have no existence outside the imagination of
the author and have no relation whatsoever to anyone bearing the same
name or names. They are not even distantly inspired by any individual
known or unknown to the author, and all incidents are pure invention.

This edition published by arrangement with Harlequin Books S.A.

® and TM are trademarks of the publisher. Trademarks indicated with
® are registered in the United States Patent and Trademark Office, the
Canadian Trade Marks Office and in other countries.

www.eHarlequin.com

Printed in U.S.A.

ABOUT THE AUTHOR

Amanda Stevens is the bestselling author of over thirty novels of romantic suspense. In addition to being a Romance Writers of America RITA® Award finalist, she is also the recipient of awards in Career Achievement in Romantic/Mystery and Career Achievement in Romantic/Suspense from *Romantic Times BOOKclub*. She currently resides in Texas. To find out more about past, present and future projects, please visit her Web site at www.amandastevens.com.

Books by Amanda Stevens

CAST OF CHARACTERS

Carrie Bishop—Searching for her friend on Cape Diablo resurrects an old demon...and awakens a long-dormant passion.

Nick Draco—His secret threatens Carrie's search for her childhood friend.

Tia Falcon—A runaway bride who escaped to Cape Diablo after leaving her fiancé at the altar. Now she's disappeared.

Trey Hollinger—A jilted groom with an explosive temper.

Nathaniel Glover—The monster who abducted Carrie and Tia when they were adolescents. He was never apprehended.

Ethan Stone—A mysterious stranger who lives in the upstairs apartment...and never shows his face.

Alma Garcia—She has lived in isolation on Cape Diablo for thirty years.

Robert Cochburn—An ambitious attorney with a taste for the finer things in life.

Zeke Trawick—His supply boat is the only way on and off the island.

Prologue

The body would start to smell soon.

I should have dumped it in the swamp right after it happened, but I was too afraid of being seen. Even on Cape Diablo, eyes were everywhere. I could feel them on me now as I lay naked in the dark. Grabbing a blanket, I pulled it over my feverish skin and tried to ignore the trickles of sweat that slid down my temples and ran back into my hair.

I hadn't slept in days. Squeezing my eyes closed, I willed myself to succumb to the exhaustion, but it was no use. My mind raced with fragmented images. I'd killed someone, but I hardly remembered the act at all. Rage had blinded me and by the time I emerged from that terrible haze, the body lay at my feet.

I could still smell the blood even though I'd scrubbed the walls and floors until my hands grew raw. It had taken me a long time to get everything cleaned up, and then I wrapped the body in several layers of plastic and tried to forget what I'd done. Told myself I wouldn't dwell on it.

And I hadn't until now. But tomorrow was Tuesday.

The supply boat ran on Tuesdays. Any visitors to the island would likely come then.

The driver would drop off provisions and passengers and wouldn't return until Friday. That would give me three whole days. Three days in which there would be no way off the island. No communication with the outside world. No one to stop me from doing what had to be done.

That was why Cape Diablo was so perfect for someone like me. A person could disappear out here and never be heard from again.

Chapter One

Carrie Bishop clung to her cap as the supply boat headed due west, into the sunset. Just minutes from Everglades City, civilization ended and the topography became a vast no-man's-land of sparkling channels that wound for miles through dense mangrove forests and swampy grass flats.

Once the refuge of pirates, the area had now become a sanctuary for modern-day smugglers bringing drugs, guns and humans across the border. Lawless and primal, it was the perfect place for a runaway bride to disappear.

Which was undoubtedly why Tia had fled to the islands after leaving her soon-to-be groom at the altar, Carrie decided as a wave bounced her up off the seat. Tia hadn't wanted anyone to find her, especially her ex-fiancé, a handsome executive with an explosive temper.

Carrie wouldn't have thought to look for her here, either, if not for the postmark on her letter. Known as the Ten Thousand Islands, the area could be extremely inhospitable to anyone without a good map, a GPS device and a can of heavy-duty bug spray.

Thank goodness she'd been able to hitch a ride on the supply boat, Carrie thought. She would never have been able to find the island on her own.

Although being miles from nowhere at the mercy of a complete stranger wasn't exactly her idea of a fun day. And the driver had certainly done nothing to put her at ease. When she'd met him earlier at the marina, he'd snatched the money from her hand with barely a grunt, his manner so abrasive that Carrie might have had second thoughts about climbing aboard if the attorney who'd leased Tia the apartment hadn't been at her side.

"Don't worry. Trawick's bark is far worse than his bite," Robert Cochburn had assured her. He'd driven down from Naples to meet Carrie in Everglades City, and to her relief, he'd decided at the last minute to make the trip out to the island with her. "Besides, he's the best driver around. He can navigate these waters blindfolded. Just relax and enjoy the ride."

If only she could, Carrie thought as she watched Pete Trawick with a wary eye. But she found the man just plain creepy. His cold, assessing gaze made the hair on the back of her neck stand on end, and the way he looked at her conjured up memories that both she and Tia had been running from for years.

Suppressing another shudder, Carrie turned to Cochburn. "How much farther?" she shouted over the roar of the outboard motor.

"We're almost there." He flashed a smile. "Beautiful country, isn't it? Florida's best-kept secret." He'd taken off his jacket and tie before they left the marina, and now with his cuffs rolled back and wind blowing through his thinning hair, he hardly resembled the conservative, for-tysomething attorney she'd first met at the marina.

When she'd talked to him on the phone the day before, he'd tried to discourage her visit to Cape Diablo, but Carrie had remained adamant. Without his coopera-tion, she would simply find her own way to the island because she wasn't going back to Miami until she'd seen for herself that Tia was okay. It had been nearly two weeks since she'd received her letter, and Carrie had grown more and more worried with each passing day.

And then there'd been that strange phone call two nights ago. It had come just after midnight, and the connection had been so weak, the voice on the other end so garbled that Carrie couldn't be sure the caller was Tia. But something in the woman's voice—a note of frenzy—had instilled a deep sense of foreboding in Carrie.

Of course, she could be overreacting. A recent break-in at her apartment had left her on edge so it was entirely possible that she was letting her imagination get the better of her.

But no matter how many times she tried to convince herself there was nothing to worry about, Carrie couldn't shake the notion that her friend was in trouble. If anything happened to Tia and she hadn't done everything in her power to help her, she would never forgive herself. It was hard enough dealing with the old guilt.

"Have you ever been to the islands before?" Cochburn shouted over the engine noise.

Carrie nodded. "Once, when I was a kid. My father brought me here on a fishing trip."

"Then you know enough not to wander too far off the beaten trail. Navigation is a nightmare down here. A novice could get lost and never be heard from again. Not to mention a certain unsavory element in the area."

"I've read about the drug smuggling that's so prevalent." Just weeks ago the news had been dominated by a story about an elderly couple who'd disappeared while sailing in the area. When their bodies had washed ashore, authorities concluded they'd been murdered and their yacht hijacked by drug smugglers.

"These waters can be extremely dangerous," Cochburn said grimly. "I'm not trying to frighten you, but I do feel the need to caution strangers to the area. If you exercise good judgment and a little common sense, you should be fine."

Carrie felt a prickle of unease at his words. Had he given Tia the same warning? "You don't need to worry about me. I'm a city girl at heart. Once I've seen that my friend is okay, I'll be on my way back to civilization."

Cochburn's gaze fell on the duffel bag at her feet. She knew what he was thinking. If she'd only come for a quick visit, why had she bothered to pack a bag?

The answer was complicated. The length of her visit depended on Tia's state of mind. She was prepared to stay for as long as she was needed, but if Tia was fine and enjoying her privacy, Carrie had every intention of turning around and heading straight back to the mainland. But judging from the tone of that letter, she very much feared the worst.

What if Tia had reverted back to her old self-destructive ways? What if Carrie was too late to save her?

What if, what if, what if? She'd told herself a long time ago that she was through playing that game, but old habits died hard.

She glanced back at Cochburn. "As I told you on the phone, I don't want to intrude on Tia's privacy. If she came out here to get away from it all, I intend to honor her wishes. At the same time, though…" She trailed off, her gaze moving restlessly back to the water.

"You're concerned about her," he said.

"It's been nearly two weeks since I last heard from her. And you said you haven't talked to her, either."

"But that's hardly cause for alarm," Cochburn said. "I only met her briefly when she signed the lease agreement in my office. There's no reason she would get in touch with me unless she had a problem with her accommodations."

"But I can't imagine why no one in Everglades City remembered seeing her," Carrie said with a frown. "She has a very distinctive face."

He shrugged. "I wouldn't read too much into that, either. Pete makes a supply run out to Diablo twice a week. The tenants never have to leave the island if they don't want to. That would explain why no one we talked to at the marina remembered your friend."

Yes, that made sense. Tia had always been a loner and normally Carrie wouldn't have given her absence a second thought. She would have assumed that Tia needed time to heal after calling off her marriage to Trey.

But the tone of her letter coming on the heels of the breakup…

And then that weird phone call…

Carrie shivered in the late-afternoon heat. "Tell me about Cape Diablo," she said to Cochburn as they approached another channel and Trawick powered down the engine, making conversation a little easier. "How did it get the name?"

"Probably the handiwork of some resourceful pirate looking to frighten away looters from his treasure," he said with a grin. "There's always been a bit of mystery associated with the island. Strange lights, phantom ships…that sort of thing. No doubt that's why Andres Santiago chose the place to build his home."

"Santiago was something of a pirate himself, wasn't he?" Tired of fighting the wind, Carrie took off her cap and rested it on her bare knee as she finger-combed her tangled hair.

"I see you've done some research."

She smiled. "A little. Tia mentioned Santiago's name in her letters. She seemed so fascinated by the family that I suppose she aroused my curiosity."

"I'm not surprised," Cochburn said. "Most everyone around here is a little weary of the story, but I can see why a newcomer might find it intriguing. Back in the late sixties and early seventies, Andres Santiago ran a fleet of boats to Central America, smuggling guns into the area and drugs, among other things, out. He built the house on Cape Diablo so that the authorities wouldn't be able to keep track of his comings and goings." He paused. "You have to wonder, though, what kept his poor wife sane, trapped on that tiny island with only small children for company."

"What was she like?" Carrie asked curiously.

"The first Mrs. Santiago died in childbirth…that's about all I know of her. But the second wife had a rather colorful past. She was the daughter of a Central American dictator who was overthrown by a military coup back more than thirty years ago. The father was later executed, along with most of his family and staff. The only two survivors were his eldest daughter, Medina, and Carlos Lazario, her bodyguard. Somehow Andres managed to get both of them safely out of the country and he brought them back here where he later married Medina. Carlos still lives on the island. He and Alma Garcia, who was once nanny to Andres's children, are the only permanent residents of Cape Diablo."

"And the Santiagos?"

Cochburn turned to stare at the spindrift

behind the boat. "The whole family went missing one night. No one ever knew what happened to them. But then…you said your friend wrote to you about the island so I'm sure she must have mentioned the disappearances."

"Yes, she did. But I'm interested in hearing the whole story."

Carrie couldn't tell if he was pleased or annoyed by her request. "There's not much I can add. The entire family vanished one night while the servants were on the mainland celebrating a holiday. When Alma and Carlos returned home just after midnight, they discovered the family missing and traces of blood in the boathouse. The authorities suspected foul play, but the case was never solved."

And thirty years later, the mystery of the missing family still had the power to fascinate.

Perhaps even to possess, Carrie thought un-easily as she remembered the strange undercurrent in Tia's last letter.

"Maybe Andres was afraid the authorities were on to him so he loaded his family into one of his boats and fled in the middle of the night," she suggested. "The blood in the boathouse could have been a ruse to throw the police off track."

Cochburn's eyes met hers. "That's an interesting theory."

She smiled at his tone. "But you're not buying it?"

"I barely remember Andres Santiago, but my father was the attorney who arranged the trust that allows Alma Garcia to remain in the house. The two of them were very good friends even though they were as different as night and day…the dashing smuggler and the straitlaced attorney." He paused, and his expression turned pensive. "I never learned how or why they became friends, but I do know that my father remained loyal to Andres to the end."

"So what did he think happened to them? If he was that close to Andres, he must have had his own theory."

"He believed that someone Andres had crossed in the past came looking for revenge or else the insurgents who killed Medina's family wanted to make sure she could never return to her homeland. In either case, my father was convinced the family met with a tragic end because if Andres was alive, he would somehow have managed to get word back to him."

Carrie mulled over the possibilities for a moment. "What about the nanny...Alma Garcia? Was she never considered a suspect? It seems she's the one who benefited most from the family's disappearance."

Cochburn grimaced. "If you call living alone on an island all these years a benefit. Alma didn't inherit the property outright, and the only monetary compensation she receives is a small monthly allowance that barely takes care of her basic needs, much less the upkeep of the house and grounds. That's why some of the property has been converted into apartments and rented out.

Her inheritance was hardly the kind of fortune that would motivate one to mass murder. Besides, my father said that she was devoted to those children. She loved them as if they were her own. She would never have done anything to harm them."

Stranger things have happened. "Why do you think she's stayed on the island all these years?" Carrie asked.

"One can only speculate, but I think at first she was waiting for the children to return. Then later, once loneliness and dementia set in, she forgot why she was there. Whatever her reason, she's remained in that house all these years, living in her own little world."

Carrie tried to imagine what the woman's life must have been like for the past thirty years, but it was hard to put herself in Alma Garcia's place. Carrie had been born and raised in Miami, and she loved the daily hustle and bustle of big-city living. As a graphic designer for a local magazine, she was used to a hectic pace. She'd go crazy living so far from civilization. "You say she's one of only two permanent residents on the island?"

"Yes, and as you can see, the area is quite isolated. If your friend came out here looking for solitude, she certainly found it."

Carrie didn't bother telling him that Tia had come to Cape Diablo for more than just solitude. She'd been running away, not only from a future with a man she no longer wanted—a man she might even have come to fear—but from a past that would haunt her for the rest of her life. Carrie knew what that was like because she shared Tia's past. The two of them had been running from the same nightmare since they were twelve years old.

"Are there any other tenants?"

"A man named Ethan Stone moved into one of the apartments a few days ago. I don't know much about him. His secretary made all the arrangements, but I gather he's a Wall Street–type suffering from a bad case of burnout."

"He has my sympathies," Carrie murmured.

"And, of course, there's Nick Draco, the carpenter I hired to do some repairs. He's staying in the old servants' quarters."

"So at the moment there are only five people living on the island," she said.

"That's right. Like I said, if your friend wanted solitude, she came to the right place."

They both fell silent after that, and Carrie turned her attention to the scenery as she tried to imagine Tia's frame of mind when she'd traveled across these same waters three weeks earlier. She must have felt desperate when she'd fled Miami, but why Cape Diablo? Carrie had never even heard of the island. How had Tia found out about it?

Perhaps a friend or colleague had told her about it, Carrie decided. It was the kind of place that would only be advertised by word of mouth. Not at all like the five-star resorts Trey was undoubtedly used to, which was probably why Tia had chosen it.

For all Carrie knew, Tia had been contemplating the trip for weeks as her wedding day approached and her jitters had turned into panic. Maybe she hadn't been able to work up the courage to call off the ceremony until faced with the inevitable.

Tia had left a note for Carrie in the bride's room, begging her to break the news gently to the distraught groom. Trey Hollinger had put up a poised front for the hundreds of guests assembled in the chapel, but once he and Carrie were alone, he'd unleashed his fury on her. She'd tried to convince herself his misplaced anger was classic kill-the-messenger syndrome, but Trey's wrath cut more deeply than that. He blamed Carrie for what happened. Everything had been fine, he'd raged, until she'd started planting ideas in Tia's head.

"I know what you did to her back then. She told me all about it…how you ran off and just left her there. And now here you

are back in her life and look what's happened. You just couldn't let her be happy, could you?"

Was he right? Had her rekindled friendship with Tia somehow set her friend back on the path of self-destruction?

Retrieving Tia's letter from her bag, Carrie quickly scanned the contents for the umpteenth time, hoping for something that would reassure her. But far from putting her mind at rest, a fresh reading only deepened her foreboding.

After the first paragraph, Tia never mentioned Trey's name. It was as if she'd put him completely out of her mind. Instead, she'd written about the island and the missing family. By the time she'd scribbled the last page, she'd begun—unwittingly, Carrie hoped—referring to the Santiagos by their given names, as if she'd known each of them personally.

I've seen photographs of the children. What beautiful little girls! I don't know why, but I feel strangely drawn to them. Sometimes I go down to the beach and try to imagine the two of them collecting shells, building sand castles, playing chase with the surf. Reyna, so quiet and shy, and Pilar, too adventurous for her own good. They remind me of the way you and I once were.

Carrie's grip tightened on the paper.

Maybe it's because of our own tragic past that I feel so compelled to find out what happened to those little girls. Did they sail off with their father and stepmother that night or did something dark and sinister befall them? Are they out there somewhere leading normal, happy lives, or do their spirits still wander restlessly through the halls of this crumbling mansion?

I know how strange all this must sound to you, Carrie. It's hard to explain, but I don't think I can leave here until I find out what happened to them. Sometimes I think I was drawn to Cape Diablo for a reason. It's as if the island itself is trying to tell me something…and it won't let me rest until I uncover its secrets.

"CAPE DIABLO, dead ahead," Pete Trawick shouted over the engine noise.

His gruff voice drew Carrie's attention from Tia's letter, and as she glanced up, she found Robert Cochburn watching her intently. The moment their gazes met, however, he smiled and jerked a thumb toward the front of the boat. "Heads up. You don't want to miss the scenery. The island is beautiful this time of day."

Carrie folded Tia's letter and returned it to her bag, then stood to get a better look at the view. Backlit by a glorious sunset, Cape Diablo shimmered on the horizon, a lush emerald green gilded by the dying light. For a moment, as the sun hung suspended in a painted sky, the island seemed bathed in gold. A glowing sanctuary that beckoned to the weary traveler.

Grabbing her camera, Carrie snapped a few shots, but as they approached the island, the sky deepened and the water turned dark, as if a giant shadow had crept over the whole area. It was a strange phenomenon, a trick of the light that seemed too much like an omen. Carrie couldn't seem to shake off a gnawing fear. The place seemed so wild and primitive. Anything could have happened to Tia out here.

As they approached the island, Carrie could just make out the red roofline of the house through the trees and to the right, an old, wooden boathouse nestled in a tiny cove.

Trawick turned the bow neatly toward the inlet and after a few moments, cut the engine. As they drifted silently toward the pier, Carrie became aware of a dozen sounds. Water lapping at the hull…the startled flight of an egret…an insect buzzing near her ear.

And, in the distance, a scream.

Her glance shot to Cochburn. "What was that?" she asked in alarm.

"A falcon, most likely." He put up a hand to shade his eyes as he searched the sky. "There it is. See it? Circling just above the treetops."

"A falcon?" Carrie asked doubtfully. "Way out here?"

"These islands are on the migration route. Maybe this one got lost from its cast as they flew north. When I was a kid, you could come out here in the spring and fall and spot dozens flying over Cape Diablo. My father said Andres found a wounded one once and nursed it back to health. He kept it in captivity for a number of years, but I suppose it was released after his disappearance. Who knows?" He gave Carrie an enigmatic smile. "Maybe the one you just heard is a descendant."

A wounded falcon seeking refuge on Cape Diablo.

Cochburn didn't seem to realize the irony, but to Carrie, it was yet one more clue as to why Tia had chosen such a remote location. If she'd known Cape Diablo was on the migratory route of the falcon, she might have taken it as a sign. She seemed so…mystical these days.

As the boat thudded softly against the rubber tires hanging from the pier, Cochburn climbed out and offered a hand down to Carrie. Gathering up her bag and cap, she grabbed his hand and let him pull her up.

They left Trawick unloading the supplies as they made their way along a trail that wound through a jungle of mangroves. In spite of the insect repellant she'd sprayed on before leaving the marina, Carrie had to constantly swat mosquitoes from her face as they emerged into what had once been a landscaped yard but was now overgrown with palmettos, bromeliads and swamp grass.

The house itself was still magnificent, a Spanish-style villa that appeared untouched by time as the late-afternoon sun glinted off arched windows and turned the white facade into gleaming amber. Carrie caught her breath. She'd never seen such a beautiful place.

But almost immediately she realized the soft light had created an illusion. A closer examination revealed the overall state of disrepair. Some of the roof tiles were missing and the salt air had rusted the ornate wrought iron trim around the windows and balconies. In dreary corners, lichen and moss inched like a shadow over crumbling stucco walls.

A subtle movement drew Carrie's gaze to one of the balconies, and as she lifted a hand to shield her eyes from the glare, she saw the outline of a woman standing at the railing looking down at them. Carrie couldn't make out her features clearly, but she had the impression of age and frailty.

And then a strange dread gripped her. As their gazes clung for the longest moment,

Carrie suddenly had an overpowering sensation that she was in the presence of evil.

Whether it was coming from the woman on the balcony or someone else on the island, she had no idea.

Chapter Two

Carrie must have made some inadvertent sound because Cochburn stopped on the path and glanced around. "What's wrong?"

"I'm...not sure." Her gaze was still on the balcony, but the woman had stepped back into the shadows so that Carrie could no longer see her. "I thought I saw someone up there."

Cochburn glanced warily at the house. "It was probably Alma Garcia. Her quarters are on the third floor. She must have heard the boat."

"It was so strange," Carrie murmured. "For a moment, I thought..."

"What?" he asked sharply.

She shook her head. "Nothing. I got the impression she wasn't too happy to see us, that's all."

He shrugged, but not before Carrie had seen something dark in his eyes. "She's not exactly thrilled with having tenants on the property, but she's harmless. Crazy as a bat, but harmless. You don't need to concern yourself with her. I doubt you'll even see her again. She keeps to herself most of the time." He turned back to the path. "Come along. Tia's apartment is this way."

Crazy as a bat, but harmless.

Hardly a ringing endorsement, Carrie thought uneasily. Just what had she gotten herself into?

Not that she was in any position to judge. She'd spent more than a few hours on a therapist's couch herself.

And Tia...

Poor Tia had her problems, as well. A precarious mental state was nothing new for her, unfortunately, which was why Carrie was so worried about her.

Tia had been emotionally fragile for years, but Carrie had hoped that she'd grown stronger since they last met. Evidently not, or she would have stayed and faced Trey herself on their wedding day.

Unless she had good reason not to.

Cochburn led Carrie around to the back of the house and through an old gate that opened into a large, central courtyard enclosed on one side by a long L-shaped wing of the main house and on the other by a freestanding, two-story pool house. At the far end was a cracked adobe wall topped with faded red tiles that matched the roof. Terra-cotta pots dotted the stone floor, but the flowers had mostly withered in the heat and the water in the pool was blackish green and opaque.

In spite of the obvious neglect, however, touches of a once-gorgeous oasis remained in the cascade of scarlet bougainvillea over the walls and in the tinkle of a nearby fountain. A lazy breeze drifted through the palm fronds, carrying the scent of jasmine and the barest hint of rain. And through an arched opening in the back wall, Carrie caught tantalizing glimpses of water undulating in the sunset like yards and yards of russet satin.

The only thing to disturb the almost total quiet was the sound of the ocean and the distant drone of a generator that supplied the island's electricity.

Carrie wanted a moment to take it all in, but Robert Cochburn seemed in no mood to linger.

"Your friend's apartment is just over there." He pointed to the pool house. Like the main house, it was white stucco with a red tile roof and a curving staircase that led up to a shady loggia on the second level. "She's on the ground floor."

"Thank you for taking the time to come out here with me," Carrie told him. "I'm not sure I could have found the right island without you. You never said, but…how did Tia know about this place?"

"She saw one of our newspaper ads,"

Cochburn said. "The same way most of our tenants hear about the apartments."

Carrie nodded. "I assumed it was something like that. Well, thanks again for everything."

He smiled. "No problem. Glad I could help."

She watched until he disappeared through the gate, then she turned to Tia's apartment. Carrie had no idea the kind of reception that was in store for her. Tia was hard to predict. She could be warm and effusive one moment, distant and brooding the next. But Carrie understood better than anyone her friend's mood swings.

Bracing herself for Tia's possible irritation, Carrie walked up two stone steps and stood in front of a set of French doors that opened onto the courtyard. Shades had been pulled over the panes making it impossible to see inside. She knocked softly at first, but when she got no response, she rapped harder and called out Tia's name.

Stepping back from the door, she

scanned the other windows, her gaze rising to the loggia. No one was about and the predusk calm that settled over the courtyard seemed ominous, as if the place had been abandoned in a hurry.

Moving back to the door, Carrie knocked again, then tried the latch. It was unlocked, which could mean that if Tia had stepped out for a few minutes, she probably hadn't gone far. Then again, maybe there was no reason to lock doors on Cape Diablo.

Carrie hesitated, not quite sure what to do. She didn't want to intrude on Tia's privacy, and yet she'd come this far. She couldn't turn around and leave without making sure her friend was all right.

Another thought suddenly occurred to her. Tia had run away from Miami with barely a word to anyone. What if she'd already packed up and left Cape Diablo?

Only one way to find out.

Taking a deep breath, Carrie pushed open the door and stepped inside the gloomy apartment.

COCHBURN GLANCED warily over his shoulder as he walked up the steps to the old servants' quarters located on the south end of the island near the swamp. He'd spotted Nick Draco on the roof of the main house when he and Carrie were in the courtyard so he thought this might be an excellent time to have a look around.

He didn't know why, but he was starting to get nervous about bringing Draco to Cape Diablo. In hindsight, he should have been a little more careful in screening the applicants who'd responded to his ad, but there hadn't been that many. And no wonder. Who in their right mind would want to spend a summer working on this godforsaken island?

Nick Draco had seemed the most capable of the lot, and when he hadn't balked over the miniscule wages being offered, Cochburn had hired him on the spot.

But he'd been second-guessing his decision ever since. For one thing, the background information Draco had provided on the application seemed a little sketchy, and for another, the guy's cold, relentless stare was the most unnerving thing Cochburn had ever experienced.

Draco had the look of a man who'd as soon slit your throat as not, and Cochburn was a coward at heart. Always had been. But he also had a vested interest in Cape Diablo—and what might be hidden here. According to local legend, Andres had left a fortune buried somewhere on the island. If Draco had come here to look for that money, Cochburn wasn't about to get caught unaware. It wouldn't be the first time a fortune hunter had wormed his way onto the island.

The outbuildings were even more dilapidated than the main house, and as Cochburn crossed the rickety porch, he glanced around in distaste. He supposed some might find the overgrown island quaint and primitive, but he detested coming out here. He preferred the yacht clubs and the exclusive condo communities in Naples.

Cape Diablo was an albatross around his neck, and he couldn't wait to unload it. Unfortunately, because of Andres Santiago's trust, that wasn't going to happen until Alma Garcia was either dead or committed. A missing tenant, however, might go a long way in convincing the authorities that the old girl needed to be institutionalized. Especially—God forbid—if evidence of foul play turned up.

With Alma finally out of the way, Cochburn would have free rein of the place. If the money was here, he'd find it before he put the place on the market, but in the meantime, he had more pressing worries.

Taking out a handkerchief, he mopped the sweat off his brow as he knocked on the door, even though he already knew the carpenter was still up at the villa. Still, he was wary enough of Draco to take precautions.

Throwing another look over his shoulder,

Cochburn took out a key and slipped it into the keyhole. When the door refused to budge, he realized that Draco must have changed the lock. Cochburn gave the knob a frustrated rattle, then withdrew the worthless key and walked over to peer into one of the windows.

"Looking for something?"

Cochburn froze. He hadn't heard so much as a twig snap in warning, and now the deep timbre of Draco's voice sent a chill up his spine. Sweat trickled down his temples and he swore under his breath. He was no damn good at this. He should have sent a professional to investigate Draco. But the fewer people who knew about the island's secrets, the better.

He gave himself a split second to recover before he turned. Whatever nerve he'd managed to recover fled at the sight of Nicholas Draco.

The younger man had taken off his shirt in the heat, and the sheen of sweat along sinewy muscles made Cochburn uncomfortably aware of the spare tire around his middle. He hadn't worked out in years, and in a fair fight against Draco, he'd be a dead man. In a dirty fight…he'd still be a dead man.

Draco propped both arms against the newel posts, but the relaxed pose didn't fool Cochburn. His muscles were bunched, as if ready to spring like a cat, and his gaze—that relentless stare—never left Cochburn's face.

"You didn't answer my question," he said softly. "Are you looking for something?"

Cochburn cleared his throat. "Yes, as a matter of fact, I was looking for you. I wanted to ask how you're progressing on the repairs."

One brow lifted. "That's funny because I could have sworn you saw me on the roof a few minutes ago."

Cochburn assumed what he hoped was a look of mild surprise. "You were on the roof? Sorry I missed you. I guess I was a little preoccupied."

"So I noticed."

Cochburn smiled in a knowing way. "She's a real looker, isn't she?"

Draco shrugged. "If you like blondes. Who is she?"

"Her name is Carrie Bishop. Actually, she's the other reason I came down here to find you. She's a friend of one of the tenants…Tia Falcon, the brunette who lives in the pool house. I'm sure you've seen her around." When Draco didn't respond, Cochburn said hurriedly, "Anyway, she seems to think that something may have happened to her friend."

"Why?"

Cochburn hesitated. "Something about a letter she received, I gather."

"And what does any of this have to do with me?" When Draco placed a foot on the porch, it was all Cochburn could do not to back away. Unfortunately, he had no place to retreat.

He moistened his lips. "I wondered if you'd seen her lately...say, in the last day or two."

Draco gave him a quizzical look. "I thought you were paying me to fix the roof, not keep tabs on your tenants."

"Yes, of course. But it did occur to me that your paths might have crossed. It's a small island. Not much in the way of distractions."

Draco's gaze narrowed. "What are you getting at, Cochburn?"

Sensing he was treading on dangerous ground, Cochburn immediately backpedaled. "Nothing. Nothing at all. I just thought I'd alert you to the fact that we have company on the island. If Carrie Bishop doesn't find her friend, she may come down here looking for her."

"Then maybe you'd better pass on a friendly piece of advice."

The edge in Draco's voice chilled Cochburn's blood. "What's that?"

If possible, the gray eyes went even

colder. "You go poking your nose in places it doesn't belong, what you might find is trouble."

"TIA? ARE YOU in here? It's me…Carrie." She paused just inside the door of the apartment to allow her eyes time to adjust to the dimness.

Slowly the room came into focus, and Carrie glanced around with interest. To the right of the French doors was a small sitting room furnished with wicker chairs and gauzy white curtains and to the left was a kitchenette. Straight ahead an arched doorway led to a shadowy hallway and presumably a bedroom and bath.

It was cool inside the apartment, which meant that the stucco walls were thick enough to keep out the heat. And sound, Carrie realized. Inside, she could no longer hear the generator.

Her gaze moved back to the sitting room. A tiny niche in one wall provided just enough space for an old ebony desk.

The surface had been neatly cleared, but the chair had been shoved back and left askew, as if someone had risen abruptly. Carrie frowned when she spotted it.

The misplaced chair was the kind of detail no one else would even have noticed, but she knew her friend too well. Tia was a stickler when it came to her personal space. Everything had to be orderly. Throw rugs positioned precisely. Pillows arranged on the sofa just so. Her tidiness was the one thing she could always control, no matter what.

So what had brought her up from the desk and driven her out of the apartment so quickly that she hadn't taken the time to straighten the chair or lock the door?

Carrie tried to convince herself she was making too much of that chair, but the premonition that had gripped her for days wouldn't let go. Something was wrong. She could *feel* it.

Had Tia's nightmares come back? Had they driven her from her own wedding and brought her here, to the almost complete isolation of Cape Diablo? Had she tried to shut them out by pulling the blinds over the windows and immersing herself in another family's tragedy?

Or was something far more sinister at work here? Had Tia inadvertently stumbled upon the answer to a thirty-year-old mystery?

Carrie turned to search the rest of the apartment. As she made her way down the narrow corridor, she became aware of a smell. Something faint. A lingering odor of decay that turned her stomach and made her heart pound in agitation.

It was only a trace. She'd watched enough crime shows to know that the stench from a dead body would be overpowering so she tried not to panic.

Tia is fine, she told herself over and over. The apartment needed airing out, was all.

But as she stepped into the tiny bedroom, her gaze darted almost fearfully around the small space. Her first reaction to the spotless condition of the room was intense relief.

"Thank God," she whispered, realizing that she had been bracing for the worst ever since she'd gotten off the boat.

Like the rest of the apartment, the room was immaculate. The bed was made and the floor free of discarded clothing. Tia's things were stored in the closet and her suitcase shoved out of the way on the overhead shelf. Everything was in its proper place, just the way she would have left it.

So why did she still feel that terrible sense of doom? Carrie wondered.

Walking over to the French door, she drew back the curtain and stared out at the overgrown garden. She unlatched the door and pulled it open, allowing a fresh breeze into the room. Almost immediately the scent from the hallway faded.

Carrie started to turn away when a movement beyond the garden stopped her.

Someone was coming up a path that led back into the man-grove forest, and for a moment, she thought it was Cochburn.

But as the man emerged from the trees, she saw that he was younger and taller than the attorney, with closely cropped hair and a lean, muscular body. He wore faded jeans and a shirt that hung open, revealing a bronzed chest and— Carrie would have sworn—the handle of a gun protruded from his low-riding waistband.

Nearing the house, he buttoned his shirt as he glanced over his shoulder. There was something oddly covert about his movements, and Carrie remembered her conversation earlier with Cochburn about the unsavory element in the area.

Quickly, she closed the door, then stepped back into the room before the man spotted her. He seemed to be heading directly toward her, but at the last moment, he veered off the path and disappeared back into the trees.

Who was he? Carrie wondered with a shiver. And why did he have a gun?

She watched for a moment longer, but when he didn't appear again, she turned and walked over to examine a framed photograph Tia had left on the dresser.

The picture had been taken at summer camp the year she and Tia turned twelve. They were both beaming with arms thrown over each other's shoulders. The two of them had been inseparable back then.

How odd that Tia had kept the photograph all these years and brought it with her to Cape Diablo. Carrie had long since put away everything that reminded her of that summer.

The knot in her chest tightened. It still hurt to see their shining faces in that snapshot and know what the future held for them. She and Tia had been so happy that day. So eager for a summer adventure.

But a week later, their lives had been changed forever. In the blink of an eye, the innocence had been lost, replaced by the kind of horror most people could hardly imagine.

The day of the abduction had started out like so many others that summer. The sun had been out. Carrie could still see the way the light dazzled off the man's wristwatch.

He'd seemed cute and harmless at first. It was only later when she'd seen that terrible tattoo on his chest that she'd begun to have an inkling of just how evil he really was.

"Don't leave me here, Carrie. Please, please don't leave me…."

She squeezed her eyes closed as Tia's desperate plea echoed through her head, followed by her own hollow promise.

"I won't leave you, Tia. I swear I won't…."

But she had left Tia. She'd left her all alone in that hellish place. Carrie had managed to get away, and the police had later told her that her escape had probably saved both their lives. But Carrie hadn't seen it that way, and neither, she feared, had Tia.

In spite of everything, though, the two of them had managed to resume their friendship, but nothing was ever the same after that summer.

It had almost been a relief for Carrie when the two of them had gone off to separate colleges and eventually lost touch. Away from Tia, the nightmares and guilt had finally faded.

Then, just a few months ago, Tia had come back into Carrie's life. She'd called out of the blue one day, shocking Carrie from the pleasant complacency her life had become.

"I'm getting married and I want you to be my maid of honor. There's no one else I'd rather have with me than you, Carrie. We've been through so much. Please say yes."

Of course, Carrie had said yes, even though she'd had some trepidation about renewing the friendship. After years of struggling to 'find herself,' she'd finally gotten her life on track. She had the job of her dreams with a local magazine, a great apartment, a small circle of friends. So what if she hadn't met that special someone. So what if at times loneliness threatened to engulf her. She'd finally put the past behind her and that was all that mattered.

Or so she tried to tell herself.

But Tia's phone call had brought it all back. The nightmares and the guilt.

Carrie had worked long and hard to exorcise her own demons, but they were always there lurking in the deepest recesses of her subconscious, waiting to undermine any intimate relationship she might have hoped to establish.

The guilt was still there, too. She'd gotten away from their abductor before he'd physically harmed her, but Tia hadn't. What must *her* nightmares be like?

They'd never talked about what that monster did to her, but Carrie knew. Deep down, she knew.

The wedding was to be Tia's exorcism. A chance to finally put the past to rest and have the kind of fairy-tale life she'd always dreamed of.

So what had happened? Carrie wondered. What had ended the dream and driven Tia away from the church that day? Had she simply gotten cold feet or had she discovered something about Trey Hollinger that had frightened her into running away?

And why had she brought the photograph—such a painful reminder of the past—with her to Cape Diablo?

A noise from the sitting room brought Carrie around with a start. Her mind flashed instantly to the man she'd seen a few minutes earlier on the path. He'd still been some distance from her so she couldn't be sure that she'd seen a gun, but the very idea that someone might be armed and dangerous on the tiny island made her hesitate at the doorway.

"Anyone home?" Robert Cochburn called from the sitting room.

Recognizing his voice, Carrie let out a breath of relief as she replaced the frame on the dresser, then walked down the corridor and through the archway.

The attorney hovered on the threshold, giving her an apologetic smile as soon as she entered the room. "Sorry to just barge in like this, but I did knock. I guess you didn't hear me." His gaze darted to the hallway behind her. "I trust you found your friend?"

"Unfortunately, no." Carrie brushed a restless hand through her hair. "I don't know where she is."

Something flickered in his eyes, a shadow that made Carrie wonder. "How did you get in here?"

"The door was unlocked." Realizing what he might think, she said quickly, "I wasn't snooping. I just wanted to make sure everything was okay. I thought Tia might have left the island for good."

"And?"

He had the oddest expression on his

face. Carrie didn't know what to make of it. "Her clothes are still hanging in the closet so I assume she hasn't gone far." She glanced over her shoulder. "There's a smell in the hallway. I think an animal might have gotten trapped in the walls and died."

Cochburn grimaced. "I wouldn't be surprised. The house is old and falling apart. I'm sure there are dozens of ways for mice and rats to get in. I can have someone check it out if you want."

"I should probably leave that up to Tia. It's her apartment."

They both walked outside then and Cochburn closed the door behind them. As they moved into the courtyard, Carrie suddenly remembered something in Tia's letter.

Sometimes I go down to the beach and try to imagine the two of them collecting shells, building sand castles, playing chase with the surf.

Reyna, so quiet and shy, and Pilar, too adventurous for her own good. They remind me of the way you and I once were.

Her gaze lifted to the upstairs windows at the back of the house. She almost expected to find Tia gazing down at her, but instead there was nothing but light reflecting off glass.

She rubbed her hands up and down her arms as she continued to stare at the windows. Someone was up there. Not Tia perhaps, but someone. Carrie was sure of it. She could feel those invisible eyes on her, and the dread she'd been fighting since she'd gotten off the boat seemed to seep all the way down into her soul.

Something bad had happened here. It was as if those lingering emotions had morphed into a physical presence, one that watched and waited and played on vulnerabilities.

She'd only felt this sensation one other time....

Don't, Carrie warned herself nervously. It wouldn't do to make comparisons.

It was just an old house. And something bad *had* happened there. It was no secret. A whole family had disappeared. Little wonder the place seemed to reek of sorrow and tragedy.

"Which bedroom belonged to the Santiago children?" she asked suddenly.

The question seemed to catch Cochburn off guard. "I beg your pardon?"

"I was just thinking about something Tia wrote in one of her letters. She seems so fascinated by the Santiago family, especially the little girls. I wondered if she might be up there for some reason."

"Oh, I doubt that."

Carrie turned at his adamant tone. "Why do you say that?"

He hesitated, then shrugged. "Because if she were up there, she would have seen you by now and come down."

"I suppose you're right."

"I really don't think there's cause for

worry," he insisted. "She's probably gone back to the mainland for a few days."

"But if that were the case, someone in Everglades City would have seen her," Carrie said.

"Not necessarily. We only talked to a few people at the marina. The place is full of tourists this time of year. Faces tend to blend together."

"But surely Trawick would have remembered taking her back to the mainland."

"Trawick delivers supplies and mail to Cape Diablo, but his isn't the only boat for hire in the area. She could have made previous arrangements with another driver. Or Carlos may have taken her back. You said she wasn't expecting you, so it's very possible that you've simply missed her."

Carrie hated to think that her trip to Cape Diablo had been a waste, mainly because she didn't know where to go from there. Searching for Tia in the Ten Thousands Islands would be like looking for the proverbial needle in a haystack.

She bit her lip. "I should talk to Carlos. And what about Alma Garcia? She was standing on the balcony when we came up. Maybe she saw Tia leave. Do you think it would be possible for me to talk to her, as well?"

Cochburn frowned as his gaze shot up to the third-story windows. "Alma…isn't exactly receptive to strangers," he said doubtfully. "Perhaps it would be better if I go up alone and have a word with her. Meanwhile, why don't you check with the other tenant? He may know where Tia's gone off to, and if not, we'll go find Carlos together."

Carrie nodded. "What did you say his name is?"

"Ethan Stone. He lives in the apartment above Tia's."

Carrie started for the stairs, then turned back when Cochburn called out her name. "Yes?"

He paused, as if preparing to broach a

tricky subject. "I don't want to sound overly dramatic, but I meant it earlier when I said that you shouldn't go wandering off on your own, even here on the island. Cape Diablo is small, but it'll be dark soon and the south end is nothing but swamp. It can be pretty treacherous if you don't know your way around."

She thought again of the man she'd seen earlier and nodded. "Thanks for the warning. I'll wait for you before I leave the courtyard."

"Good. I'll meet you back here in a few minutes."

They separated, and as Cochburn headed for the main house, Carrie walked up the stairs to the second-floor apartment and knocked on the door. A fly buzzed past her face and she swatted it away as she knocked a second time. Finally she gave up and headed back down the stairs to the courtyard.

In spite of Cochburn's warning, she was tempted to strike out on her own to look for

Tia. Carrie hated feeling so helpless, but she supposed the attorney was right. It would be dark soon and she didn't know the terrain. She wouldn't be of any use to Tia if she got herself lost or injured in the swamp.

Standing at the edge of the pool, she stared into the murky water and wondered what she *could* do. Was it time to go to the police?

And tell them what, exactly?

It was doubtful they'd treat Tia as a missing person. She'd run away from her wedding to come here to the island of her own free will.

The letter Carrie received had been a bit strange, but certainly nothing the police would construe as evidence. And as for the midnight phone call, Carrie wasn't even certain it had been Tia's voice on the other end of the line. The police would probably argue that Carrie had been too quick to jump to conclusions. And they might very well be right. What if she'd

launched a wild-goose chase because of
nothing more than an overwrought imagination?

Maybe she *wanted* Tia to be in trouble
so that she could ride to the rescue and
clear her conscience once and for all.

*Okay, enough with the psychoanalyz-
ing,* Carrie chided herself. She'd once paid
a therapist a fortune to do exactly that....

Her thoughts scattered as she caught sight
of something in the pool. The water was so
dirty she could barely see through it, but
something white gleamed on the bottom.

It was probably nothing more than reflected light, but for a moment it looked as
if...

No! It couldn't be.

But it was.

A body lay on the bottom of the pool.
Carrie could just make out the outstretched
arms, and her hand flew to her mouth as
her heart slammed against her chest in
horror.

Chapter Three

Tia!

Without thinking, Carrie kicked off her shoes and prepared to dive into the murky water, but someone grabbed her arm and yanked her back from the edge. She spun in shock, her gaze colliding with her captor's. She recognized him at once. He was the man she'd seen earlier from Tia's bedroom.

Fear shot through her as she tried to tear her arm from his grip. "Let me go! Someone's in the water!"

He held her fast. "Take it easy, okay? It's not a body."

"But I saw—"

"Trust me, you don't want to jump in that water. Just stand back."

Releasing her, he bent to pick up a metal pole that had been discarded near the side of the pool. Plunging it into the filthy water, he dragged the bottom where Carrie had seen the body. As he parted the water and stirred away dead leaves, she caught another glimpse of the outstretched arms.

Sick with dread and fear, she watched him maneuver the pole beneath the lifeless form and pull it up to the surface.

He was right. It wasn't a body. He was able to lift it too easily. But Carrie couldn't stop shaking even when she saw that what he'd snagged with the pole was an old shirt.

Stepping back up to the edge, she peered into the water, praying that nothing else was down there. But the flash of white she'd spotted earlier had indeed been nothing more than fabric. Somehow the shirt must have floated open on the bottom of the pool, making her think that she was seeing arms and a torso.

Behind her, the man tossed the pole out of the way, and the loud clang of metal against stone caused Carrie to jump.

She turned in embarrassment. "You must think I'm an idiot."

"It was an honest mistake."

His voice was deep and strangely unsettling. And his eyes…

My God, Carrie thought. She'd never seen a pair of colder, bleaker eyes.

Except…

She blinked away the memory as she found herself at a complete loss for words. She didn't usually rattle so easily, but after days of worrying about Tia and then spotting what she thought was a dead body in the pool…it was all taking a toll on her poise.

And now that deadly stare.

She glanced away. "I'm not usually so excitable. But I came all the way out here to see my friend and no one seems to know where she is." She paused, then said apologetically, "Not that you have any idea what I'm talking about. Maybe we should start over. I'm Carrie Bishop."

She started to extend her hand, then thought better of it. Did she really want to make physical contact with a man whose eyes seemed to pierce right through her soul? "You're not by chance Ethan Stone?" she asked hopefully.

His expression remained stoic, but a shadow flickered in his eyes. "Not even close. I'm Nick Draco."

Nick Draco. Carrie rolled the name around in her head. It sounded familiar for some reason. Had Tia written about him in her letter? "Do you live on the island, Mr. Draco?"

"For as long as the job holds out."

Ah. Now she knew who he was. He was the carpenter Cochburn had told her about. That would certainly explain his dark suntan and the muscles she could see bulging through his shirtsleeves.

"Mr. Cochburn mentioned that he'd

hired someone to renovate the house." She glanced up at the crumbling mansion. "You certainly have your work cut out for you. It's a beautiful place, but it looks as if it could take years to restore."

"I'm here to plug a few leaks. I doubt Cochburn has much more than that in mind."

His gaze never left Carrie's face. Tiny shivers raced up and down her spine. She couldn't remember the last time a man had affected her so strongly. She wanted to look away again, but his eyes were almost hypnotic.

"Why did you think I was Stone?" he asked suddenly.

She shrugged. "I was looking for him earlier and when I turned and saw you standing there, I guess I just assumed you were he. Sorry for the confusion."

"No harm done."

Without another word, he started to turn away, but Carrie said, "No, don't go. I'd like to ask you something."

He waited reluctantly, one brow lifting as his gaze connected with hers again.

"As I said, I came out here looking for my friend…Tia Falcon. Do you know her?"

"Brown hair…about your size?" His eyes dropped slowly, then lifted. "I've seen her around."

Carrie tried to ignore the ripples in the pit of her stomach. "Do you remember the last time you saw her?"

He thought for a moment. "A few days ago, I guess."

"Are you sure it wasn't more recent?" she asked anxiously.

He frowned. "Could have been, I guess. I can't say for sure. I stay pretty busy around here. I don't keep track of who comes and goes."

Somehow Carrie doubted that. She had a feeling Nick Draco missed very little of what went on around him. "But it's such a small island. If a boat came out here to pick her up, you would have seen it, surely? Or at least heard the engine?"

"Not necessarily. Depends on where I happened to be at the time." He studied her for a moment. "You seem pretty worried about your friend. Was she expecting you?"

"No. I didn't have any way to let her know that I was coming."

"Then maybe she went back to the mainland for a few days."

"That's what Mr. Cochburn said." Carrie wrapped her arms around her middle. "But I just can't help feeling that something is wrong."

His gray-blue eyes watched her intently. "Are you suggesting she met with foul play?"

The blunt query took Carrie aback even though she'd been dancing around the same question in her own mind for days. She'd had a premonition that Tia was in trouble ever since she'd received that strange phone call in the middle of the night. No, before that even. The uneasiness had started when Tia had fled her own wedding.

Up until that point Carrie hadn't wanted to give credence to her doubts about Trey Hollinger, but when she thought back to the way his temper had exploded after learning he'd been left at the altar, she was hard-pressed to believe he hadn't played some role in Tia's running away.

His anger had been over the top that day, and Carrie suspected that if she'd been alone with him, his rage might even have escalated into violence. She hated to admit it, but he'd frightened her. And she didn't frighten easily these days. Or at least, she rarely let herself succumb to her fears.

She couldn't help wondering if Tia had witnessed that side of Trey, too. Had she glimpsed something in her handsome fiancé that had scared her so badly she hadn't dared face him on their wedding day? Had she been running from Trey when she came out here?

Was she *still* running from him?

Carrie had a vision of Tia's battered body lying in the bushes somewhere. Or underwater, her wrists and ankles tied to weights.

After everything she'd been through to come to that fate...

A fist of fear closed around Carrie's heart. For one split second, she thought she might actually be sick.

"Are you okay?"

She swallowed past the lump in her throat. "I'm just worried about Tia. Mr. Cochburn thought that she might have gotten a ride back to the mainland with Carlos Lazario. Have you seen him today?"

"No, but Carlos couldn't have taken her back. His boat has a broken fuel pump. He's waiting on a part from the mainland."

"I...see." Until that moment, Carrie hadn't realized how desperately she'd been hoping for a logical explanation for Tia's absence. Now the last door had been slammed in her face, and she didn't know what to do.

"Has it ever occurred to you that your

friend might not want to be found?" Nick Draco asked quietly.

Carrie glanced up. "Why would you say that?"

He shrugged. "People usually come to a place like this for one of two reasons. They're either running away or they're hiding from something."

Or someone.

Carrie wanted to ask which category he fit into, but she held her tongue.

"Maybe she knew you'd come here looking for her so she left."

"She couldn't have known I was coming. I didn't tell anyone." Too late, Carrie realized her mistake. She was miles from civilization and she'd just admitted to a stranger that no one knew where she was. She'd said nothing of her plans to anyone at the magazine and her parents were in Europe for a month. And her friends…Carrie hated to admit it, but they probably wouldn't miss her, either. They were accustomed to her sometimes eccentric behavior.

Her gaze shot to Nick's and she saw something flash in his eyes. Something that made the chill inside her deepen.

"What about Cochburn?" he said. "You must have said something to him."

"I talked to him yesterday on the phone. He agreed to meet me in Everglades City. But...you don't think he would have warned Tia that I was coming, do you?"

"I wouldn't put it past him."

Carrie bit her lip. "But that still doesn't explain why no one here saw her leave."

"Maybe she planned that, too." He paused, then shrugged. "Sorry I can't be of more help."

He turned to walk away and Carrie let him go this time. But his final words echoed in her ears. *Maybe she planned that, too.*

Carrie wanted to call after him that he didn't know what he was talking about. Tia wouldn't worry her like that, but how well did she know Tia these days? They hadn't communicated in years until she'd called out of the blue about her engagement. And then she'd skipped out on her wedding leaving Carrie to clean up the mess with Trey.

Maybe Nick Draco was right. Maybe she should just accept the fact that Tia had left Cape Diablo without a word to anyone, because she'd done it before.

After all, running away was what they both did best.

"DID I SEE YOU OUT HERE with Nick Draco?" Robert Cochburn hurried across the courtyard toward Carrie. "He wasn't bothering you, was he? What did he want?"

His anxious tone took Carrie by surprise. "Bothering me? Why would you think that?"

He glanced over his shoulder at the gate through which Nick had disappeared a few minutes earlier. "He's only been here a couple of weeks. I don't know that much about him, but he can be a bit intimidating. I hope he didn't frighten you."

"You sound as if you don't trust him," Carrie said uneasily.

Cochburn rubbed the back of his neck. "I hired him to do odd jobs around this place. You don't exactly get the cream of the crop for that kind of work."

"I thought you said you hired him to renovate the house." His tone worried Carrie. What was he not telling her about Nick Draco?

"I hired him to do what he can as long as the money holds out. And there isn't much of that," Cochburn added with a grimace.

Carrie hesitated. "Did you know that he carries a gun?"

"A *gun?*" Alarm flashed in Cochburn's eyes. "How would you know that?"

"I saw him earlier coming up the path to the garden. He had the gun tucked into his jeans and I got the impression that he was trying to conceal it with his shirt."

"A gun, you say." Cochburn grabbed his handkerchief and mopped his forehead.

"I take it you didn't know he was armed," Carrie said.

"No, but I'm sure it's just a precaution- ary measure. After all, Cape Diablo is a long way from civilization. No phones. No communication with the outside world. In many ways, this area is like the last frontier. It pays to be on guard."

The last frontier.

An apt description, Carrie thought wor- riedly. Cape Diablo was even more prim- itive and remote than she'd pictured. She couldn't imagine what Tia had been thinking. Obviously, she'd wanted a place where she could get away from it all.

And Nick Draco? What had brought him to the island?

It was pretty apparent that Cochburn didn't trust the man, and after staring into those cold eyes, Carrie could see why. But she decided to let the matter drop for the moment. "Were you able to talk to Alma Garcia?"

"Yes, but I didn't get much out of her.

Her lucid days are getting fewer and farther between, I'm afraid."

"She didn't say anything about Tia?" Carrie asked in disappointment.

"No, nothing. What about Ethan Stone? Was he any help?"

Carrie sighed. "He's not home. Or at least, he didn't answer my knock."

"Hmm." Cochburn's expression turned pensive as he gazed up at the second-floor apartment. "Kind of a coincidence that both he and your friend are away at the same time. You don't suppose they could have gone off somewhere together, do you?"

"I don't think so. You said he'd just moved in a few days ago, and Tia hasn't been here much longer. I don't see her going off with someone she just met." Trust issues aside, Tia had never made friends that easily. Even before the abduction she'd been painfully shy and reserved, always content to let someone else make the first move.

Carrie suddenly remembered the way that Tia had described the two Santiago children in her letter. *Reyna, so quiet and shy, and Pilar, too adventurous for her own good. They remind me of the way you and I once were.*

Yes, Carrie had been the adventurer, the instigator, the one who had always prodded Tia out of her comfort zone.

If she hadn't encouraged her to leave the campgrounds that day…

If she hadn't stopped to flirt with the young man in the van…

Carrie blinked away the memory and tried to focus on the here and now. She'd learned a long time ago not to dwell in the past. All it did was keep you trapped in fear.

"What about Draco?" Cochburn was saying. "Did you ask him about your friend?"

"Yes, but he couldn't remember the last time he'd seen her. He also told me that Carlos couldn't have given her a ride back to the mainland because his boat has a broken fuel pump."

"Well, that's that then." Cochburn took a final swipe at his forehead, then stuffed his handkerchief back into his pocket. "I really don't know what more you can do here. I think your best bet is to go back to the mainland and wait until she contacts you again."

"And if she doesn't?"

"Then you can charter a boat and come back out here." He glanced at his watch. "Right now, though, we should probably get down to the dock. As soon as Trawick gets the supplies unloaded, he'll want to head back to Everglades City."

"But I thought you said he could navigate these islands blindfolded," Carrie protested. "Surely a few more minutes won't make a difference."

Cochburn gave her a troubled glance. "Navigation has nothing to do with it. I told you earlier, there are a lot of rumors about Cape Diablo. Trawick won't want to be anywhere near the island come night-fall. And if we let him take off without us, we'll be stranded here until he comes back on Friday. I don't know about you, but I don't relish the prospect of being stuck here for the next three days."

"I suppose you're right," Carrie murmured although she hated the idea of leaving without seeing Tia. What if she was still on the island? What if she was lying hurt somewhere? What if she needed Carrie to come and find her?

But Cochburn had a point. It would be dark soon, and she didn't know the terrain well enough to go out searching on her own. There really wasn't anything more she could do here on the island tonight.

She sighed in defeat. "I left my bag in Tia's apartment. As soon as I get it, I'll be ready to leave."

Cochburn nodded. "Good. I'll head on down to the boat and make sure Trawick doesn't leave without you."

"Thanks."

Carrie hurried across the courtyard and let herself into Tia's apartment. When she didn't see her bag in the living area, she realized that she must have left it in the bedroom.

As she started down the hallway, she noticed that the smell from earlier had disappeared. She paused as the back of her neck prickled in warning.

Something was different. It wasn't just that the odor had faded. She could feel a draft coming from the bedroom as if a window had been opened to allow the place to air out. But she'd closed the garden door earlier. She was sure of it.

Carrie took a cautious step inside the bedroom, then stopped cold. For one heart-stopping moment, she thought someone stood just inside the French door. She had a sudden image of the woman she'd seen earlier on the balcony staring down at her. The evil she'd sensed then crept back over her, but she realized that it was only the curtain blowing in the breeze.

But someone had been in Tia's bedroom. What if the intruder was still there?

Carrie's gaze shot to the closet. The door was shut. Had she closed it earlier? She didn't think that she had. Ever since she was little, she'd had a thing about leaving closet doors open so that she could see if anyone—or anything—was hiding inside.

What if *he* was in there?

She could picture him inside, crouched in a dark corner, waiting to spring at her the moment she opened the door. But in her imagination, just as in her nightmares, her abductor's face had morphed into the horned monster on his chest. She could almost feel those glowing red eyes on her now.

Don't be ridiculous, she told herself firmly. Even though the kidnapper had never been caught, the odds that he had somehow found them fourteen years later and followed them to the island were remote. He was probably dead by now or incarcerated for another crime. He couldn't be here on Cape Diablo, as fitting as the name might be. Carrie was letting her imagination run away with her again.

Maybe she hadn't done as good a job at putting the past behind her as she'd thought.

Taking a deep breath, she edged toward the door.

Don't let him see your fear, a little voice warned her. *That's what he wants.*

Trying to tamp down her panic, Carrie grabbed the door and flung it back, jumping when it hit the wall with a bang. Quickly she stepped inside the closet and flipped on the light switch.

No one was inside.

She let out a shaky breath. Okay, she really was letting her imagination run wild here. Monsters in closets? *Come on.* She'd been cured of that particular phobia years ago.

Or so she'd thought.

Switching off the light, she backed out of the closet, closing the door behind her with firm resolve. As she turned to look for her bag, she saw something shiny on the floor near the dresser.

Frowning, she walked over and picked it up, then gasped in recognition. It was the silver friendship pendant she'd given Tia before they left for camp that summer. Carrie ran her hand over the inscribed *Friends*.

The other half of the breakaway heart, engraved with the word *Forever*, was buried someplace in her jewelry box back home. She'd never worn hers again after that summer, but she couldn't bring herself to get rid of it, either. Instead, she'd hidden it away and hadn't thought about it for a long, long time.

Until now.

She clutched the chain in her fist. The necklace hadn't been there earlier. She would have seen it on the floor. Which meant that someone *had* come in after she left.

But who? And why?

And then realization crashed over her, and her heart thudded in excitement. The necklace hadn't been dropped by accident. It had been left on purpose by someone who knew that Carrie would understand its significance.

Tia!

She was still on the island!

For some reason she couldn't come to Carrie openly. Maybe she was in hiding or in some sort of trouble. Maybe she was on the run. Whatever her motive, it was obvious she needed help. The necklace was a message, a desperate plea that only the two of them could interpret.

"Don't leave me here, Carrie. Please, please don't leave me."

Chapter Four

Carrie stood at the end of the dock, clutching a key to Tia's apartment in her hand as she watched Trawick's boat disappear from view. Cochburn had reluctantly given her a spare key after he'd tried to talk her out of her plan, but Carrie had remained adamant.

Now, however, as the sound of the engine receded in the distance, she almost wished she'd succumbed to his persuasion. She'd just stranded herself on an island in the middle of nowhere for three whole days.

Was she out of her mind?

The initial shock of finding the necklace

had worn off by now and panic was starting to set in. She couldn't swear with any certainty that the necklace had been left as a message. Maybe it *had* been there earlier and she'd somehow overlooked it. Maybe the wind had blown open the garden door. It was entirely possible that no one had come into the apartment after she'd left, and now she'd isolated herself on Cape Diablo for no good reason.

What if she got sick or hurt out here? How would she get help?

And even if Tia really was still here and in some kind of trouble, how was Carrie supposed to find her? She didn't even know where to start looking for her.

Obviously, she hadn't thought this through, but when had that ever stopped her? She'd always had a bad habit of leaping before she looked.

In hindsight, instead of overreacting and jumping to conclusions, she should have gone back to Everglades City and filed a missing person report with the local authorities. Or insisted that the police accompany her to the island and mount a full-scale search.

She should have done something, *anything* other than isolate herself on the same island from which Tia had gone missing. How stupid was that?

Now it was too late. The boat was gone, and as the sound of the engine faded away, an almost preternatural silence fell over the island.

It's okay, Carrie told herself firmly. She'd done the right thing. The police in Everglades City probably wouldn't be of much help anyway. She had no proof that Tia was in trouble. There was no sign of foul play in her apartment, nothing to suggest that she hadn't left the island of her own accord.

Besides, the boat would be back in three days. That would give her ample opportunity to conduct a thorough search on her own. Maybe her instincts were right and the necklace really had been a call of distress from Tia.

If there was even a slight chance that she was in trouble, Carrie would do everything in her power to help her. She wouldn't turn her back on her no matter what. She'd left her behind once, and neither of their lives had ever been the same. She couldn't do it again. This might be her last chance to make things right.

"That wasn't too smart, you know."

Carrie wheeled at the sound of Nick Draco's voice. He'd moved up behind her so silently she hadn't heard him approach, and even when she turned, she still couldn't see him in the fading light. The long shadows of twilight seemed to absorb him.

And then he disengaged himself from the trees and started toward her.

Carrie's first impulse was to back away from him. To turn and run as far and as fast as she could in the opposite direction. She was still wary of everyone on the island, but especially Nick Draco. He seemed to have a strange, unsettling effect on her.

She moistened her lips. "I beg your pardon?"

"You should have gone back to the mainland when you had the chance." His voice was dark and menacing, yet somehow seductive...like the island itself. Carrie shivered as he continued toward her. "With Carlos's boat out of commission, there's no way off the island."

"I realize that, but I wasn't ready to leave," she said with what she hoped was a negligent shrug.

"Like I said, not a smart move." Nick's gaze pierced through the dusk and slid along her nerve endings. Carrie didn't want to stare at him, but she couldn't seem to glance away.

"And why is that?" she demanded.

"Haven't you heard? People have a bad habit of disappearing around here."

Carrie's heart skipped a beat. Was he warning her...or threatening her?

A chill shot through her veins as he came even closer. He'd taken off his shirt and draped a towel over one shoulder as if he were on his way down to the beach for a swim. Even in the vanishing light, she could see the hard definition of his shoulders and chest, the smooth ripple of muscle down his abdomen.

He looked lean and raw, not at all the sort of man she was normally attracted to. She went for the more offbeat, artsy types. Nick Draco's overt sexuality drew her and repelled her at the same time.

And then as he slipped the towel off his shoulder, she saw the tattoo that had been hidden beneath. It was some kind of symbol that she didn't recognize.

She caught her breath as she instantly thought of another tattoo. She hadn't been able to look away from that one, either, as the man had grabbed Tia and held her at knifepoint. *"Don't run,"* he'd warned Carrie, *"Or I'll slit your little friend's throat. You don't want that on your conscience, do you?"*

The memory was so vivid that when

Nick took another step toward her, she gasped and jumped back. She couldn't help herself.

He froze, obviously puzzled by her reaction. "What's wrong? You look as if you've seen a ghost."

She couldn't answer him for a moment. Her heart was beating too fast. In spite of all her hard work, she suddenly found herself trapped in the past.

"Hey, are you sure you're okay?"

Don't let him see your fear, her inner voice warned her. *That's what he wants.*

Carrie's head snapped up. "You...startled me, is all. I didn't hear you come up before, and I guess I'm still a little jumpy."

She could feel the power of his eyes and trembled, wanting to run away, but knowing she had to stand her ground. She'd vowed a long time ago that no one would ever make her feel weak and helpless again. Not her abductor. Not Nick Draco. *No one.*

He watched her steadily. "I didn't mean

to startle you. I came down to see the boat off. I was surprised to find you still here."

She ignored the pulse that was suddenly throbbing in her neck. "What did you mean when you said people have a bad habit of disappearing around here?"

He shrugged. "It happened a few years ago. A family disappeared off the island and no one ever knew what happened to them."

Carrie frowned. "I know about the Santiagos. Are you sure you weren't talking about something more recent?"

"Like your friend, you mean?" He used the towel to slap at a mosquito on his leg. "I don't consider her missing. I thought we agreed that she's probably gone back to the mainland."

"That's what you and Mr. Cochburn seem to want me to believe," Carrie said coolly.

"You can believe whatever you want," he said in a dismissive tone. "I simply offered an opinion. I think your friend probably got bored on the island and took off for civilization. Maybe for a few days, maybe for good. Either way, I don't think you're going to find what you're looking for on Cape Diablo."

Why did she suddenly have the feeling he was no longer talking about Tia? "Maybe you're right," Carrie said. "Maybe Tia has gone back to the mainland. But I won't have any peace of mind until I know for certain that she's not here."

"So what's your plan?"

Carrie drew a breath, trying to calm her still-racing heart. "Search the island, of course. Every square inch if I have to."

He gave her the longest stare. When he finally spoke, his tone remained casually indifferent, but somehow Carrie thought there was an underlying tension in his voice. For some reason, her presence on Cape Diablo mattered to Nick Draco, but she had no idea why. "Take my advice and at least wait until daylight."

"Why? The sooner I search the island, the sooner I'll find her."

"Assuming she's still here," he said with a frown. "Cape Diablo may be small, but there's a lot of rugged ground to cover, especially on the southern end."

"You mean the swamp?"

He lifted a brow. "You know about that?"

She nodded. "Cochburn warned me about it earlier."

"Did he? Well, good for him. But the swamp's not the only thing you have to look out for."

"What do you mean?"

He gave her another enigmatic look. "Do you know what a bog is?"

"Isn't it the same thing as a swamp?"

"Not exactly. A bog is a marshy area that's like a quicksand pit. The only safe way to get across is to lie on your belly and crawl to the other side. But the problem is, you may not know you're in it until you feel the mud sucking at your feet. By then it's too late. You're already stuck and the harder you struggle, the quicker you sink."

Sink? Carrie glared up at him. *Good lord!* Was he serious? "Why do I get the feeling you're trying to discourage my search?"

"I'm just trying to keep you out of trouble. People come out here from the city and think this place is like a resort. It's not. It's primitive and dangerous, and if you're not careful—" He paused, his gaze raking over her in the darkness. "You may need someone to come looking for you."

CARRIE WAS AMAZED at how quickly twilight turned into night. By the time she got back to the apartment, the courtyard already lay in deep shadow.

In spite of Nick's warning, she still felt an urgency to begin searching for Tia immediately. For all she knew, hours or even minutes could make a difference.

But as strongly as her instincts warned her that her friend was in trouble, her common sense prevailed. Even with a flashlight, the unfamiliar terrain would be difficult to navigate with any degree of confidence. And as much as she hated to admit it, her conversation with Nick had spooked her. She didn't want to get stuck in a bog…if there even was such a thing.

She shivered now as she remembered his warning. His ominous tone only added to the menacing vibe of the island. There was something about Cape Diablo after dark that made Carrie want to retreat inside and lock her doors.

The rustling leaves in the courtyard sounded like whispers; the pounding surf, the echo of a human heartbeat. The whole island seemed personified somehow, as if it were a living, breathing entity.

Carrie could feel the panic welling inside her again, but she tamped it down. She was here for a reason. She couldn't let her fears get in the way.

She'd proven a long time ago that she was a survivor. She wouldn't let Cape Diablo—or her imagination—drag her back to the darkness again. No more cowering in corners for her. No more lying awake at night to ward off the nightmares. She'd vanquished her demons once before. She could damn well do it again...for her sake and for Tia's.

Refusing to retreat inside, Carrie stood in the doorway, her gaze lifting to the towering facade of the main house where a single light glowed from one of the third-floor windows. As she watched, the window went dark.

She started to glance away, then paused when she realized that rather than extinguishing the light, someone had stepped in front of the window.

She could see the outline of a woman against the backdrop of light, and Carrie suddenly had the disturbing notion that Alma Garcia was staring back at her. She couldn't see the woman's features, but she felt those dark eyes on her, and Carrie remembered Cochburn's assessment that Alma's lucid days were getting fewer and farther between.

Carrie couldn't help but wonder how thirty years of seclusion on Cape Diablo would affect one's sanity.

Why had the woman remained on such a remote island after the Santiago family disappeared? Why had she exiled herself here for so long? Was she still waiting, as Cochburn speculated, for those missing children to come home?

Carrie was surprised at how intriguing she found the old mystery, but unlike Tia, she couldn't allow herself to get caught up in it. She'd come to Cape Diablo to find her friend. Whatever secrets the Santiago family had left on the island would have to remain hidden for now.

But what if the missing family was the reason for Tia's disappearance?

What if she'd discovered something that had put her in danger?

The last line of Tia's letter came back to Carrie now: *It's as if the island itself is trying to tell me something…and it won't let me rest until I uncover its secrets.*

So she'd noticed it, too. The sense that Cape Diablo was a living, breathing entity with a heartbeat, a pulse and a dark, restless soul in which decades of secrets lay hidden.

"Looks like we may be in for some rough weather later."

Nick's voice startled her so violently that Carrie jumped. She'd been so caught up in her thoughts that she hadn't heard him approach. She didn't like his habit of sneaking up on her. She didn't like the way her pulse raced in recognition.

"Sorry," he murmured. "I didn't mean to startle you. Again."

"That's the third time today," Carrie said accusingly. "Maybe you should think about putting a bell around your neck."

"What if I just cough or clear my throat? Would that work?"

"Maybe." Her breath quickened at his nearness.

She didn't believe in love at first sight. She wasn't even sure she believed in love at all. She'd had sex but never intimacy, and somehow over the years, she'd managed to convince herself that was the way she wanted it.

But Nick Draco's mere presence awakened a restless yearning inside her that she couldn't explain. She didn't want to be attracted to him, but she was. She didn't want to be afraid of him…but she was.

She had a bad feeling that he could hurt her in ways she'd never even imagined. Not physically, perhaps, but something far, far worse.

Sensing her unease, he paused, reluctant to close the remaining steps between them. He almost seemed worried that he might scare her away.

He wouldn't. Not physically. But there were other ways to run, other ways to hide.

Their gazes met and the night, silent moments earlier, suddenly came alive with the pounding of Carrie's heartbeat.

"The sky's perfectly clear," she finally said in response to his initial comment.

"For now. But something's in the air. Can't you feel it?"

"What?"

He glanced up at the sky, then back down at her. His eyes seemed to burn through the darkness. "Electricity."

Yes, of course, she felt it. But it seemed to Carrie a brewing storm had very little to do with the way the back of her neck tingled.

He carried a large box underneath one arm, and after another moment, he moved forward and set it down at her feet.

"What's that?" she asked in surprise.

"Some of the supplies Trawick left. If you're staying until Friday, you'll need provisions."

The gesture caught Carrie off guard. Kindness wasn't something she expected from a man like Nick Draco.

"Thanks, but I'm sure I can manage." Although she wasn't certain of that at all since she'd yet to check Tia's refrigerator and cupboards.

"Suit yourself. But I'm leaving it here just the same. If you don't take it, the rats will."

Carrie grimaced, remembering the unpleasant smell earlier in Tia's apartment.

"In that case, I accept," she said gratefully. "But I hope you're not running yourself short."

"I've got plenty." He paused. "What I said about people disappearing from the island…I'm sorry if I frightened you. That wasn't my intention. I only meant to warn you."

Somehow the considerate and conciliatory Nick Draco was even more perplexing than the dark, intimidating stranger Carrie had met previously. It made her wonder if he was playing some kind of game with her. "You don't need to worry about me," she tried to say evenly. "I can take care of myself."

"That may be true under normal circumstances, but Cape Diablo isn't Miami. It would be a mistake to think that it is."

"Your concern is duly noted, Mr. Draco—"

"Nick."

She shrugged. "I'm not quite as helpless as you seem to think, and I'm not the type to be easily frightened away. Until the boat returns on Friday, I intend to use my time here on the island to find out what happened to my friend. If that makes you uncomfortable for some reason..." She left the innuendo hanging in the air as she bent to pick up the box of provisions.

"I know you're worried about your friend," he said softly. "I still say she's probably gone back to the mainland—"

"Then why are her clothes still here?" Carrie cut in. "Why did no one see her leave the island?"

"But if you're that determined to search the island, then I'll help you," he continued as if she'd never spoken.

His proposal stunned Carrie. "Why?" she blurted. "If you really think that Tia is somewhere on the mainland, why would you waste your time helping me look for her here?"

"Because you're going to do it with or without my help, and I don't think you have any idea what you're getting yourself into. You go off on your own and you might end up with a twisted ankle or... worse."

Carrie frowned at the slight emphasis he placed on the last word. "What century are you living in?" she asked in annoyance. "Women do all sorts of things these days. We're actually quite capable," she added with an edge of sarcasm.

"I didn't mean to imply otherwise. I've known some exceptionally capable women..." His voice trailed off, leaving Carrie to wonder about those women. "But at the very least, I can show you where the dangerous areas are so that you can avoid them."

Carrie hesitated, not certain she wanted to take him up on his offer. Going off with Nick Draco just might be more dangerous than wandering around alone. "Let me ask you something." She turned to set the box inside the door, then straightened and folded her arms. "Why is it that you seem so certain I'll run into trouble here on the island, but you're perfectly willing to believe that Tia is somewhere safe and sound on the mainland? What if she went off on her own for some reason? What if she ended up with a twisted ankle…or worse?" Carrie said, using his words. "Isn't that a possibility?"

He shrugged. "Anything's possible. But in your friend's case, I don't think it too likely. I saw her around a few times, and she didn't strike me as the adventurous type. In fact, I don't think I ever saw her wander any farther than the courtyard."

"But she obviously *did* go farther than the courtyard. And you didn't see or hear her leave," Carrie pointed out.

"True. Which is why I'm willing to concede that there's a remote possibility she could still be on the island. And why

I'd like to help you search for her tomorrow if you have no objections. If you're as worried as you say you are about her, you should welcome another pair of eyes and ears."

Maybe, but could she trust him? For all Carrie knew, Nick Draco might be the reason that Tia had gone into hiding.

"At least let me show you where the bog is," he said, as if reading the hesitation in her eyes. "You don't want to stumble into it by accident."

Carrie finally nodded. "All right. Since you don't seem to have much faith in my abilities," she added.

He gave her another long appraisal. "I don't even know you, so don't take it personally. I just don't have much faith in human nature in general. I don't dare," he muttered under his breath.

What a strange thing to say, Carrie thought as she watched him disappear through the arched opening in the back wall.

And then with something of a shock,

she realized that a complete stranger had managed to capture in three little words what she had been feeling for years.

She didn't have much faith in human nature, either. She'd never had an intimate relationship, never let herself fall in love, never opened herself up in any way...because she didn't dare.

NICK RESISTED the temptation to glance over his shoulder as he strode through the gate. Carrie Bishop was an attractive woman, but unfortunately, she was also going to be one big pain in the ass.

Already, he resented the amount of time and energy he'd have to expend to keep her out of trouble. He didn't get off playing tour guide nor could he afford to spend every waking hour keeping tabs on her. But at the moment, he didn't have a choice.

As he headed down the path to the out-buildings, he begrudgingly admitted that his irritation probably stemmed from more than just the inconvenience her presence presented. She was blond and gorgeous and that pissed him off.

Not that he couldn't avoid temptation, but he didn't like having to. He'd been on this island for too damn long. He was sick of the peace and quiet. Sick of the isolation. He was ready for the job to be over and done with so that he could get back to civilization. Patience had never been his strong suit, and the boredom of surveillance was starting to wear on his nerves.

But his orders from JIATF East—the Joint Interagency Task Force located in Key West—had been clear and succinct. No arrests. No heroics. No blowing his cover. He was there only to observe and, if possible, substantiate a recent intelligence report that identified Cape Diablo as a probable drop point in the drug trade.

In the weeks since Nick's arrival in the area, he'd found very little in the way of concrete proof, and until he had what he needed, it was imperative that he maintain a low profile. He couldn't afford to arouse suspicions with a lot of questions, and the last thing he needed was for Carrie Bishop to drag local law enforcement to the island to start snooping around.

Somehow he had to keep her away from the cops while he found a way to convince her that her friend was safe and sound on the mainland. But he'd have to be careful not to push her too hard. She didn't come across as the overly trusting type or one who would back down from her convictions. If anything she would dig her heels in even harder.

So what if Tia Falcon really was in trouble?

The question niggled at him, but Nick shrugged it off.

Not my problem, he thought grimly as he continued down the path. He had his orders.

Skirting the edge of the swamp, he made his way toward a slight incline that overlooked the water on the south end.

The natural harbor on this side of the island was the perfect setup for smuggling, which was no doubt why Andres Santiago had acquired Cape Diablo all those years ago. The water was deep enough to accommodate large yachts and separated from the mainland by hundreds of mangrove islands. To the west, the open waters of the Gulf provided a glittering speedway for the go-fast boats that were notorious for eluding Coast Guard detection.

After insuring that everything was quiet in the harbor, Nick headed around to a smaller cove nestled between the harbor and the old boathouse where Carlos Lazario lived. A canopy of mangrove branches camouflaged the tiny inlet. Nick would never have known it was there if he hadn't scoured every square inch of the island on his arrival.

Peeling back the branches, he saw that the powerboat he'd spotted three nights ago was still there.

He had no idea who it belonged to or

when it had arrived, but the fact that someone had gone to a great deal of trouble to conceal the boat could only mean one of two things: either someone on the island was prepared for a quick getaway…or Cape Diablo had a visitor who didn't want to be seen.

Chapter Five

After Carrie put away the supplies, she went back to the bedroom to make sure she hadn't missed any other clues that Tia might have left for her.

She searched for several minutes, then satisfied that she hadn't overlooked anything, she rechecked the lock on the garden door and propped a chair under the knob for good measure. She realized that in taking the extra precaution she might be barricading Tia from her own apartment, but that was a chance she had to take. If Tia really was in some kind of trouble, the threat could be coming from someone on the island and Carrie didn't want to risk having that same someone creep into the apartment while she slept.

Going back out to the living room, she sat down at the desk and began to search through the drawers. The first one yielded nothing of consequence, but the second contained a file folder with several copies of newspaper articles.

Tia must have printed them off the Internet, Carrie thought as she thumbed through the pages. Most of the articles were about the Santiago disappearances, and she was once again reminded how caught up in the mystery Tia had sounded in her letter. Obsessively so.

But as Carrie continued to skim through the articles, her attention was caught by one that wasn't related to the missing family or to Cape Diablo. It was the article and photograph that had run in the *Miami Tribune* announcing Tia's engagement to Trey.

Carrie stared at the picture for several long moments, thinking again what a striking couple they'd made and how well suited they seemed for each other, at least in appearances. Tia's delicate, ethereal beauty had complemented Trey's polished sophistication so well.

He was a handsome, charming man, no question. Attentive and courteous, he'd seemed like the perfect fiancé. And yet from the moment Carrie had first met him, she'd sensed something in him that left her cold. He was a little too charming, a little too doting, a little too perfect. Even so, she would have been willing to overlook her misgivings if he'd made Tia happy.

But that was the odd thing. Carrie had never been convinced of Tia's happiness. They'd met for lunch right after she first phoned Carrie, and instead of gushing about her handsome fiancé and her upcoming nuptials, Tia had turned the conversation time and again back to Carrie. She'd wanted to know every detail of Carrie's life and seemed fascinated by her position at the magazine.

Her own job as an executive assistant with an insurance company was deadly boring, she'd confided. So boring in fact that she didn't plan to return once she was married. Which was fine by Trey because he preferred a more traditional wife anyway.

Nothing wrong with that, Carrie kept telling herself. Her mother had been a stay-at-home wife and Carrie didn't know of anyone who worked harder or had a more satisfying life. She respected her mother's decision and she respected Tia's, too—providing it really was *her* decision. But at the time, she'd gotten the distinct impression that it was Trey talking, not Tia.

And then the way he'd blown up at the wedding…Carrie just couldn't get that out of her head. His temper had been explosive and terrifying, and for a moment, he'd seemed so out of control that she'd actually feared for her life.

She would never forget that look in his

eyes. The rage and contempt that had contorted his handsome face into something ugly and feral…

Shaken by the memory, Carrie got up and walked over to the window to glance out. Moonlight shimmered off the pool, drawing her gaze to the murky water. For a moment, she could have sworn she saw something floating on the surface, but it was gone in the next instant, leaving her to conclude that it must have been her imagination.

She suddenly felt chilled just the same.

Rubbing her arms with her hands, she tried to tell herself that what she'd glimpsed was nothing more than a shadow. Nothing was in the water. She was letting the island get to her.

She was beginning to understand the strange tone of Tia's letter. Cape Diablo had an unsettling effect. Remote, primitive and dangerous, the island seemed possessed somehow. Perhaps not by ghosts, but by memories.

Turning away from the window, Carrie

walked back over to the desk and stared down at the engagement picture. She didn't want to believe that Trey had harmed Tia, but it happened all the time. Violence against women was all too common these days, and the more Carrie thought about it, the more Trey Hollinger seemed to fit the mold. Handsome and gregarious on the outside, cold and manipulative on the inside.

A noise from overhead jolted her from her reverie, and Carrie glanced upward. Someone was walking about upstairs. Wherever Ethan Stone had been earlier when she'd knocked on his door, he was obviously home now and making no effort to conceal his presence.

Should she go up and talk to him?

Carrie glanced at her watch. It was early, only a little after nine, and he was obviously still up. He might not be able to shed any light on Tia's whereabouts, but if there was even a remote possibility that he had seen her leave the island and could put Carrie's mind to rest, she was willing to risk his annoyance at her intrusion.

Slipping out of the apartment, she paused in the courtyard to study the sky. The wind had picked up and the air felt heavy with rain.

So Nick had been right earlier. They were in for a storm.

Casting a wary glance at the pool, Carrie hurried up the outside stairs and knocked on Stone's door before she lost her nerve.

No answer.

That's odd, she thought with a frown.

She knew that he was home because she'd heard him moving about. So why didn't he answer his door?

Cochburn had said the man was an executive suffering from burnout. Perhaps he avoided all forms of human contact these days. But what if she was in trouble and needed help? Would he still ignore her? Had he ignored Tia's plea for help?

Carrie lifted her hand to knock again,

then froze as a premonition swept over her. She had the strangest sensation that Ethan Stone—or someone—was standing on the other side of the door, just inches away, listening and waiting.

Her heart started to pound as she suddenly experienced an overwhelming sense of danger. She didn't understand it nor did she try to rationalize it. Instead, she whirled and rushed down the stairs, only pausing when she reached the bottom.

Slowly she turned back to stare up at the apartment.

What was going on here? Why had she panicked? Why had she felt such a crushing need to get away from that place?

For a split second, she hadn't been able to breathe, her fear was so strong.

You're overreacting. Go back up there. Face your fear. It's the only way to conquer it.

Carrie placed a foot on the next step and might have continued up the stairs, but the sound of a closing door somewhere nearby stilled her again. Instinctively, she melted into the shadows, her eyes glued to the loggia above her.

But the sound hadn't come from the upstairs apartment. Someone had come out of the main house.

Carrie's heart pounded as a shadow glided past her in the courtyard.

It was Alma Garcia.

At least…she thought it was Alma. She looked much younger than the impression Carrie had had of her earlier. Her long hair was loose and blowing in the breeze, and the filmy gown she wore billowed about legs that were still shapely and slender. She walked with her shoulders back and her head held high, her bearing almost regal.

It was almost as though she were a different woman tonight.

Her sudden presence in the courtyard took Carrie by surprise. Cochburn had said earlier that she hardly ever left her third-floor quarters. And yet here she was.

Carrie suddenly remembered the feeling she'd had earlier when she spotted Alma on the balcony. She'd had the oddest impression of being in the presence of evil, and she waited now for the eerie sensation to strike her again.

But all she felt at the moment was curiosity and a little apprehension that she might be spotted.

Pressing herself against the wall, she watched as the older woman went to stand at the edge of the pool. For the longest moment, she stared into the murky depths as if mesmerized by something in the water.

What does she see? Carrie wondered anxiously. The same shadow that she'd glimpsed earlier?

Or something else…something that lay hidden beneath the surface…

Carrie had the uncomfortable notion that she was witnessing a moment meant to be private, but she couldn't bring herself to make her presence known. She remained huddled in the shadows at the bottom of the stairs as Alma continued to contemplate the water.

Then, as if sensing she wasn't alone, Alma turned toward the stairs. Carrie's pulse quickened even though she knew she hadn't made a sound or a move, and she didn't think that Alma could see her in the shadows.

The older woman's gaze seemed to move reluctantly up the steps to the loggia, and as she peered into the darkness, her hand lifted slowly to her chest and she made the sign of a cross.

The blood in Carrie's veins turned to ice.

My God, she thought desperately. So Alma Garcia felt it, too. The danger that seemed to emanate from the upstairs apartment.

Was that the source of the evil she'd sensed when she first arrived on the island?

Who was this Ethan Stone person and why was Alma Garcia so afraid of him?

Why did Carrie instinctively fear him even though she'd never set eyes on him?

It didn't make sense. Nothing on this godforsaken island made sense. She should have listened to Robert Cochburn and gone back to the mainland for the night.

Now it was too late. She was trapped until the boat came on Friday.

Carrie fought back the panic that mushroomed inside her. She didn't know why, but she thought it was important that Alma not see her.

Finally, the woman tore her gaze from the loggia and gliding toward the back wall, disappeared through the archway.

A few moments later, the murmur of voices drifted through the opening, but Carrie couldn't make out the conversation. She had the impression they were speaking Spanish and wondered if Alma had gone to meet the elusive Carlos Lazario.

She didn't hang around to find out.

Dashing across the courtyard, she let herself into Tia's apartment and locked the door behind her.

I STOOD AT THE FOOT of the bed and watched her sleep. She stirred restlessly, turning her head from side to side on the pillow as if in the throes of some terrible nightmare. Or as if on some level she intuited my presence.

Breathlessly, I waited for her to open her eyes and see me, but she didn't wake up. I remained safe. For now.

But her nearness excited me, and after a while, I began to fantasize about how I would kill her. It would be so easy to do it while she slept. I could press a pillow to her face or plunge a knife deep, deep into that throbbing heart....

I did neither.

She remained safe. For now.

I watched her for a few minutes longer, then turned and made my way out of the apartment the same way I'd come in.

ON SOME LEVEL, Carrie knew that she was dreaming, but she couldn't force herself to wake up, even when she felt that terrible presence staring down at her. She was trapped in a nightmare, trapped in the past and no matter how hard she fought her way to the surface, the darkness kept pulling her back under.

She was twelve years old again and back in that terrible place. She could feel the shadows closing in on her, and the smells... dear God, those horrible smells...

SOBBING, TIA CLUNG to her in terror. Carrie tried her best to soothe her. "We'll find a way out of here. Don't be scared, okay?"

"Don't leave me here, Carrie. Please, please don't leave me."

"I won't leave you. I swear I won't."

But in spite of her brave words, Carrie had no idea how she would get them out of that place alive.

Why, oh why, had she talked Tia into leaving the campgrounds with her? Why had she insisted that they stop and talk to a stranger?

But the young man in the van hadn't exactly been a stranger. He worked for one of the venders who brought supplies to the camp several times a week. Carrie and the other girls had seen him unloading the trucks and thought he was cute. They'd all giggled and whispered when he smiled back at them, and Carrie had been flattered when he singled her out with a wink.

And then when he stopped his van to offer her and Tia a ride back to camp, Carrie had wanted to accept because she knew it would make the other girls jealous.

Tia had balked, though, and that's when the man got really angry at them. He jumped out of the van and grabbed Tia by the hair. Jerking her head back, he thrust a knife under her throat and warned Carrie to do as he said or he'd kill Tia and make her watch.

So Carrie did as he told her. She climbed into the back of the van, and he shoved Tia in behind her. He bound their hands and feet with duct tape, then locked them in and drove for what seemed like hours.

By the time they stopped moving, it was dark outside. He opened the back doors of the van and cut the tape from around their ankles, then ordered them to get out.

As Carrie struggled to her feet, she glanced around helplessly. They were somewhere in the woods, but she had no idea which way the camp lay.

And anyway they'd driven for hours. They had to be miles away from where they'd set out. Even if she and Tia managed to get away, where would they run to?

Forcing them inside a tumbledown cabin, he locked them in a dark room that reeked of urine, sweat and other scents Carrie didn't dare name. She knew instinctively that they were not the first girls he'd brought there, and she wondered desperately if any of the others had managed to get away.

A filthy mattress had been thrown on

the floor, and after a while, Tia curled up and fell asleep. Carrie was exhausted, too, but she didn't dare sleep. She had no idea when the man would come back. She had to use this time to find a way out.

The door was bolted from the outside and solid enough that she couldn't budge it. The only window in the room was covered with a wire mesh screen that was screwed into the walls. Some of the glass panes were broken out, and she could hear animal noises from the woods. The eerie night sounds made her yearn for home. For her mother's arms tightly around her and her father's gruff voice assuring her that she was safe.

But her parents weren't even in the country. Her mother had accompanied her father on one of his business trips while Carrie was away at summer camp. Even if she could find her way home, no one would be there.

They'd be back soon, though. When they heard that Carrie was missing, they'd rush home, but it might be too late. Carrie might never see them again.

She brushed tears from her face and tried to concentrate on searching the room for a way out or even a weapon. She was smart. She could do anything she set her mind to. Everyone said so. She could find a way out of here if she kept looking....

Footsteps!

He was coming back!

Carrie scrambled back over to the mattress and lay down next to Tia just as the door flew open. She squeezed her eyes closed and pretended to sleep, but she could feel him standing at the foot of the mattress, staring down at them.

Slowly she opened her eyes. She couldn't help herself. He'd taken off his shirt, and in the moonlight that filtered in through the broken window, she could see clearly the large tattoo on his chest. It looked like some kind of demon or monster.

A scream rose to her throat, but Carrie knew instinctively that was what he wanted so she bit down on her tongue and remained silent.

But as she stared up at him, that terrible image on his chest somehow became more real to her than the man's flesh-and-blood face. His features were diminished by moonlight, but that monstrous face seemed to come alive. Carrie couldn't look away. It was the monster who laughed at her fear. The monster who grabbed Tia and hauled her to her feet.

"Don't!" Carrie screamed. "Please don't hurt her!"

But he only laughed harder as he dragged Tia toward the door. "Don't you worry," he said in a raspy voice that sent chills down Carrie's spine. "I've had my eye on you ever since you got to camp. Your name's Carrie, right?"

When she said nothing, he grinned and pulled Tia back against his chest. Her eyes went wide with terror as he pulled out the knife.

"Please," Carrie begged. "Let her go."

"Now don't you worry," he taunted. "You'll have your turn soon enough." His tongue flicked out and he licked the side of Tia's face. She started to whimper as her eyes pleaded for help.

Carrie took a step toward them, but the man made a sawing motion with the knife across Tia's throat and Carrie froze.

"Just relax," he said with a grin. "I'll be back for you in a little while. I always did like saving the best for last."

He turned then and shoved Tia out the door. She landed hard on her knees and cried out. Carrie sprang toward the door, but the sight of his naked back stopped her cold. Giant, coiled horns were tattooed on his shoulders.

Horns that belonged to the monster on his chest...

Carrie had never seen anything so terrifying in her life, and she couldn't hide the sound of horror that slipped through her lips.

Slowly he turned to face her. "What's

the matter? You scared, Carrie?" He ran the knife blade down his chest, bisecting the monster's face with a long, thin cut.

As the blood trickled from the wound, he lifted a hand and smeared it across his face, then sucked his fingers. And all the while, he never took his eyes off Carrie. They seemed to glow now just like the monster's, and she shrank back from him.

He laughed again. "Well, you better be scared, little girl. You have no idea...."

Chapter Six

Carrie came awake with a start. She bolted upright in bed, her hand at her throat as her heart pounded in terror. For a moment, she thought she was still back in that locked room, but as the fog of sleep cleared, she realized it was just the old nightmare coming back to haunt her. She hadn't had a dream that real in years.

Collapsing against the pillow, she placed her hand on her chest and tried to calm her racing heart. She didn't want to dwell on the images the dream had awakened. She'd put them behind her a long time ago. Monsters and demons didn't exist. Not the kind that had been tattooed on her captor's chest anyway. He hadn't been possessed. He hadn't had special powers. He'd been nothing more than a sick, perverted man who preyed on young girls.

The graves the police had found underneath his cabin proved how sick he truly was. Carrie and Tia had been lucky, one of the federal agents had told her. They could have simply disappeared and never been heard from again…like all those others.

Agent McDougal had been wrong, though. Carrie had been lucky, but Tia…

Carrie squeezed her eyes closed. If she let herself, she could still hear her friend's screams.

But she'd become very good at blocking them out…just as she had on that night fourteen years ago.

Trembling, she pulled the covers up to her chin and lay with her eyes wide-open. She wouldn't think about the dream. She wouldn't think about the past. She wouldn't even think about Tia.

Instead, she lay on her back and stared up at the ceiling, focusing all of her attention on the patterns made by the lightning. She could still hear thunder, but it sounded a long way off, and she realized the storm had already passed over. She'd slept through most of it.

After a while, her eyes began to droop, but she promised herself she wouldn't fall back asleep. She wouldn't take a chance on her subconscious dredging up more memories. But the harder she fought it, the heavier her lids became.

Finally, as gray light began to filter into the room, Carrie closed her eyes and slept. She dreamed again. When she awakened to sunlight streaming in through the window, she realized that the images still fresh on her mind were not the demons from her past, but of Nick Draco.

She'd been dreaming about him when she woke up. He'd stood at the foot of her bed gazing down at her. Those steely eyes had beckoned to her and almost against Carrie's will, she reached for him.

Then she'd seen the tattoo on his left shoulder. In her dream, the strange symbol had writhed and twisted, re-forming itself into something with red, glowing eyes that mesmerized her. Carrie couldn't move. She couldn't even scream. She was powerless against those eyes....

Then somehow he was in bed with her, moving over her, and as Carrie looked up, she saw that it was his eyes that were glowing, his eyes that were hypnotic, his eyes that left her powerless....

She blinked, trying to banish the remnants of both dreams as she swung her legs over the side of the bed and headed for the shower. She refused to think about Nick Draco in a sexual way. The man was a stranger and a dangerous one for all she knew. She might have no control over her dreams, but she could certainly corral her waking thoughts from straying in his direction.

Although that might not be so easy since she'd agreed to let him show her around the island this morning. He'd probably be along at any moment, and Carrie intended to be fully dressed when he showed up.

Climbing out of the shower a few minutes later, she hurriedly dried off and pulled on the spare jeans and T-shirt she'd brought with her from the mainland. Then she went out to the kitchen to scrounge for something to eat.

She'd discovered last night when she put away the supplies Nick brought over that Tia had left a fairly well-stocked refrigerator and pantry, which only strengthened her belief that her friend had not meant to leave for an extended time. Why would she stock up on supplies if she hadn't planned on coming back soon?

Grabbing an apple, Carrie walked over to the window and raised the shades to allow in the light. She was shocked to see the dilapidated state of the house and courtyard in the harsh glare of sunlight. Yesterday, by sunset, the flaws had been camouflaged, but now Carrie realized that the place was in much worse shape than she'd originally thought.

But even the crumbling walls and overgrown gardens couldn't completely hide the graceful lines and stately elegance. She could easily imagine how the estate must have looked when Andres Santiago had first built it.

And what an undertaking that must have been, ferrying supplies, men and equipment back and forth from the mainland. Construction would have taken months, perhaps years, but when it was completed, Santiago had created a magnificent domain far from the prying eyes of civilization. And the authorities.

As Carrie's gaze lifted to the roof, she saw that Nick was already hard at work replacing some of the damaged tiles. He was shirtless once again, his skin gleaming and bronzed in the sunlight.

And she was instantly reminded of the way he'd looked in her dream. Of the way she'd reacted to him.

She watched him for a moment longer, admiring his grace and agility as he moved about the sloping roof with little regard for his safety. Then with a resolute sigh, she turned and walked away from the window.

Paging through the articles that she'd found last night, she decided that it would probably be a good idea to read every single one of them. She might find something that would at least give her a clue as to Tia's state of mind. It was a long shot, of course, but she had to start somewhere.

She sat down and was soon engrossed in the articles. The more she read about the island, the more fascinated she became with its history. Cape Diablo had a long tradition of violence, first as a hideaway for pirates and then as a base for Andres Santiago's smuggling operation.

She remembered the theories Robert

Cochburn had said his father formulated after the family's disappearance. Either someone who'd crossed paths with Andres had come looking for revenge or the rebels that overthrew Medina's father wanted to make sure that she never returned to her homeland.

Carrie wondered if there might be another possibility. What if Andres had killed his family, buried them somewhere on the island, and then fled in the middle of the night? What better way to disappear than to make the authorities believe that you were dead?

The only thing Carrie knew about Andres was that he had apparently operated with autonomy outside the law. She had a hard time believing that such a man could have cared deeply for his family. He'd isolated them on this island and left them vulnerable to his enemies. They'd been completely at his mercy, and it was hard for Carrie to imagine a man like that being a good husband and father.

But a murderer?

She could certainly believe it of Trey Hollinger. Why not Andres Santiago? Who knew what had happened that night thirty years ago? The only survivors were Alma Garcia and Carlos Lazario, and if they hadn't spoken up by now, they would probably both carry whatever secrets they harbored to their graves.

Even as caught up as Tia had apparently become in the Santiago mystery, it was unlikely she'd stumbled across something that had put her life at risk. If the authorities hadn't solved the case in thirty years, how realistic was it that an amateur sleuth had uncovered new evidence?

Carrie started to return the clippings to the drawer when she realized that one of them must have fallen out of the folder the night before. It was lying faceup on the bottom of the drawer, and as she reached for it, she scanned the headline: Child Molester Freed From Prison; Conviction Overturned on Technicality.

Carrie dropped the paper on the desk as if it were in flames.

It was just a newspaper article, she told herself desperately. It couldn't mean... It just wasn't possible...

Their tormentor was long dead by now. *Or incarcerated for another crime.*

How many times had she told herself that? How many times had she tried to convince herself that if he was in some prison, he'd never get out?

But what if he had?

Carrie forced herself to pick up the article and study the accompanying photograph. The man's name was Adam Pritchard. It didn't ring any bells, but there was no reason why it should. The kidnapper had gone by the name of Nathaniel Glover, but the authorities had learned that he'd used a fake ID to get the job at the camp. No one knew who he really was.

He'd probably stumbled across the dilapidated cabin by accident and used it as his lair. The owner of the property had told the police he hadn't been out there in years and since it was located miles from the main road, Glover had been able to come and go as he pleased without arousing suspicion.

And that far off the beaten trail, no one had heard the screams.

Carrie waited for the shock of recognition to hit, but she felt nothing. The man in the photograph didn't match her memory of their abductor. The bald-headed, muscular inmate bore little resemblance to the tall, lanky young man who'd charmed a bunch of bored twelve-year-old girls at summer camp.

But fourteen years was a long time. Assuming he'd been in his midtwenties at the time of the abduction, he'd be nearing forty now. And according to the article, he'd served time in a Florida state prison for the past ten years. A decade of incarceration would change a man. From everything Carrie had read, child molesters received brutal treatment in prison.

Could he be the same man?

Tia must have thought so. Why else would she have printed the article? Why bring it with her to Cape Diablo unless it held some significance?

But how had she come across it in the first place? Did she scour the Internet on a regular basis for some clue as to their abductor's identity and whereabouts?

Somehow the thought of that chilled Carrie to the bone. She wanted to believe that both she and Tia had moved on, but who was she kidding?

The abduction would always be with them. It had shaped their lives and made them who they were. There was no getting away from that summer no matter how hard they tried. No matter how many demons they faced down.

Carrie checked the date of the article. It had run only a few days before Tia's wedding. Was that why she'd taken off? Did she think the kidnapper would somehow find her again?

What if he had?

What if he'd followed Tia to Cape Diablo? What if he'd used her disappearance to lure Carrie here?

She'd managed to escape him, but Tia hadn't. He'd taken Tia with him when he fled the cabin, and she'd later been found in a motel room near the Alabama border. The FBI even suspected that he was the one who'd made an anonymous call to the local authorities, but his motives were puzzling, especially after the grisly discovery under the cabin.

He'd killed all the others. Why had he let Tia go?

Unless he thought that he could use her somehow.

Carrie thought back to the conversation she'd overheard between her parents and the FBI profiler who'd come to interview her. After he'd finished with Carrie, she'd been sent out of the room. The adults had no idea she was listening in at the door.

"Mr. and Mrs. Bishop...I hate like hell to have to say this, but...I think the only

reason he let Tia go was because he thought he might be able to use her somehow. She's his link to your daughter. It's my belief that Carrie was his target all along, and when men like that become fixated on someone, the obsession can last for years...."

Carrie hadn't listened to the rest. She'd run back to her room, crawled into bed, pulled the covers over her head and tried to pretend that she was safe. She didn't want to think about that man coming back for her. She didn't want to imagine what he would do to her if he found her, but she couldn't stop herself from dreaming about him.

He'd tormented her sleep for years, and then one day the nightmares had stopped. They hadn't returned until now.

Carrie shoved the article inside the folder and closed it. No reason to look at it again. It wasn't him.

It wasn't him.

She was making too much of a random article that probably meant nothing at all.

But she knew that it did. Nothing about any of this was random. Tia had deliberately run away on her wedding day, deliberately chose Cape Diablo as her hiding place, and she'd deliberately sent Carrie that letter knowing that she would come.

Just as she had deliberately left the necklace on her bedroom floor knowing that Carrie would stay.

She was trying to tell Carrie something, perhaps even to warn her that they were in terrible danger. Everything that had happened was like a puzzle piece, but Carrie still didn't have a clue how to put it all together.

And she had a bad feeling that time was running out.

SHE DIDN'T LOOK so good, Nick thought when Carrie answered his knock the next morning. Even her suntan couldn't disguise the dark circles underneath her eyes. She looked as if she hadn't slept a wink the night before.

He noticed something else about her, too. Her blue eyes were the exact shade of the flowers that used to grow in his grandmother's garden. He was surprised he hadn't picked up on that before. He was used to committing even the smallest detail to memory.

Maybe he was slipping, but at thirty-three, he could hardly blame the oversight on old age. It was more likely that the monotony of the island was getting to him. Making him careless. Making him think of Carrie Bishop in ways he had no business imagining.

He tried to look away, but she seemed to have some kind of hold on him. In the split second before either of them said anything, he found himself thinking about the most inane things. Like what she would look like with one of those blue flowers tucked behind her ear.

He had no idea if his grandmother's garden was even still there. He hadn't been out to the old place since she'd moved out.

She was in a nursing home now, and his brother, Matt, had sold her property to finance his drug habit.

But that was another story, Nick thought bitterly. He hadn't seen his brother in years, either. The trek out to the prison had long since gotten old.

Besides, he'd pretty much given up on Matt. His brother was what he was, and the fact that the same blood flowed in their veins was a reality Nick had come to terms with a long time ago. No use dwelling on the past.

His gaze flicked over Carrie, and his thoughts moved on to *her* past. She had a quality about her he couldn't quite define. She seemed tough and vulnerable at the same time. Remote and yet oddly appealing.

Something had happened to her. Something bad. He'd seen that haunted look on too many faces not to recognize it for what it was. She was a woman with demons. That much was clear to him.

He'd told her once that people came to

Cape Diablo because they were either running from something or hiding out. He couldn't help wondering if she'd come to the island on the pretext of searching for her friend. Maybe Carrie Bishop was running from something, too.

"I was beginning to think you might not show up," she said coolly as she stepped back to allow him to enter. "I thought we were going to get an early start."

He shrugged. "Sorry, but I had to work this morning. I finished as fast as I could, and now here I am, ready to rock and roll if you are."

"Just let me grab my camera," she said, hurrying over to the desk.

His gaze drifted over her jeans and sneakers. "I'm glad to see you brought sensible clothes. You'll need them where we're going."

She turned, still checking her camera. "Yes, well, I always try to be prepared for any contingency."

"Good to know."

She glanced up then and their eyes met for another brief moment before she quickly looked away. "I'm ready now. We should probably get started before it gets too hot."

Nick wondered if she even noticed the double entendre. Things were already getting a little warm between them whether she wanted to acknowledge it or not. He'd seen the way she looked at him last night...the way she'd shied away from him as if she didn't quite trust what she was feeling.

He was attracted to her, too. Another time, another place, he might have made a move. But for now he'd have to stick with his plan to get her off the island as quickly as possible.

Out in the courtyard, she turned to him again. "Where should we start?"

He jerked a thumb toward the opening in the back wall. "We'll go down to the beach, head north and make our way around the entire island."

She nodded, but as she turned toward the light, he noticed again how exhausted she looked.

"Are you sure you're up for this?"

"I told you before, I'm fine," she said curtly, then gave him an apologetic smile. "Sorry. I didn't mean to snap, but...I'm running on a short fuse this morning. I didn't sleep well last night. I guess it takes a while to get accustomed to the island. But I still want to do this. The sooner we finish our search, the sooner I'll know if Tia is still here or not."

"And if she isn't?"

"Then I'll just have to keep looking."

Nick paused. "You two must be awfully close for you to go to all this trouble because of a letter."

"How do you know about the letter?" she asked with a frown.

"Cochburn mentioned it yesterday. He said you seemed concerned by something your friend had written. Is that right?"

"It wasn't so much what she wrote as

her tone," Carrie said. "But it's not just the letter that has me worried. It's…" She trailed off on a shrug.

"It's what?"

She shook her head. "You wouldn't understand because you don't know Tia the way I do. We've been friends since we were four years old. We've been through a lot together, and there was a time when I probably knew her better than anyone. I know she's in trouble because I can feel it. I can't explain it any better than that."

"I'm not one to discount intuition," he said. "But once we search the island, there won't be anything else you can do here. Maybe you should think about going home. What if she's been trying to reach you there? Have you even thought of that?"

"Of course, I've thought of it. I'll check my messages as soon as I return to the mainland, but in the meantime, I'm stuck here until Friday. I may as well make the most of it."

"Even if it means hiking through a snake-infested swamp?"

She winced. "Yes, even that."

"Must be nice to have a friend like you."

She gave him a horrified look, and Nick thought, *What's that all about?*

"I'm…not anything special," she said hesitantly. "Wouldn't your friends do the same for you?"

"They might, if I had any."

"You don't have friends?"

He shrugged. "I travel around a lot. Never in one place for too long. It's hard to make any long-term relationships when you don't know where you'll be from one day to the next."

Something flickered in her eyes and then she nodded. "I understand. It's easier that way."

For an uncomfortable moment, Nick had a feeling that she understood a little too much. She was easy to talk to, which surprised him. She didn't come off as particularly warm and engaging. Just the opposite in fact. Most of the time she seemed pretty adept at keeping her distance.

And yet there was something in her eyes that made him want what he hadn't had in years.

Chapter Seven

The search took the better part of the morning. Starting on the western side near the beach, they circled north, past the tumbledown boathouse where Carlos Lazario lived and the pier which faced east toward the mainland.

As they made their way through the thick, junglelike growth in the interior, Carrie called out Tia's name over and over, but after a while she gave up and tried to concentrate instead on searching for clues.

And on keeping up with Nick. She'd always considered herself in reasonably good shape, and for the first hour or so, his brisk pace hadn't been a problem. But trudging through the thick undergrowth had taken a toll on her stamina.

By the time they emerged from the woods, she was hot, thirsty and tired. Pausing in the shade of a banyan tree, she bent over and placed her hands on her knees to catch her breath.

Nick glanced over his shoulder, then stopped and backtracked to where she stood. "You okay?"

"Just a little winded. I'm not used to walking so much in the heat."

"You should have said something. We could have stopped at any time."

"I'm fine." She straightened, trying to prove that she really was. "I want to cover as much territory as possible."

He glanced at his watch. "It's almost noon. Maybe we should call it a day. It's going to get even hotter from here on out, and we've pretty much been over the whole island. There's not much left to see."

Carrie surveyed their surroundings.

"Where are we anyway? I'm turned around."

"We're on the south side of the island." Nick nodded toward the trail. "If you stay on this path, it'll take you into the swamp. Veer to the right and you'll end up at the harbor."

"I remember reading about Cape Diablo's natural, deepwater harbor," Carrie said. "Andres Santiago used it for smuggling drugs into the country. That's probably what attracted him to the island in the first place. That and the seclusion."

"Sounds like you've done some research," Nick commented.

She shrugged. "Tia's letter made me curious. She seemed fascinated by the island and the Santiago family. Do you know much about their disappearance?"

"Just the usual talk." Nick broke off a tiny twig and peeled away the bark with his thumbnail. "There's a lot of mystery surrounding it, but unfortunately, disappearances aren't that uncommon when drugs are involved."

His matter-of-fact tone sent a chill up Carrie's spine. "I suppose that's true," she murmured. "It's still tragic, though. Especially when children are involved. I wonder if Andres even considered the dangers of being so far away from civilization when he bought this island. The isolation may have protected him from the authorities, but it also made him vulnerable to his enemies."

"People in the drug trade are a ruthless breed," Nick said grimly. "I doubt Santiago was any different. He may have thought of the dangers to his family, but he was probably more concerned by how the island would benefit his operation. And Cape Diablo is damn near perfect for smuggling. You've got cover from all those mangrove islands to the east and a quick getaway on the open waters of the Gulf to the west."

So the strategic location of the island hadn't escaped Nick's notice. Was it merely a casual observation or had he also done some research?

Carrie couldn't help wondering again what had brought him to Cape Diablo. As much as she wanted and needed to trust him, she couldn't shake the notion that there was more to Nick Draco than met the eye.

And she couldn't forget that she'd seen him with a gun her first day on the island. Maybe the weapon was a precautionary measure as Cochburn had suggested, but Carrie didn't think it a good idea to let down her guard around Nick.

"How long did you say you've been here?" She tried to ask casually.

"A few weeks."

"You must have been here when Tia arrived. Did you talk to her?"

He leaned a hand against the trunk of the tree as he stared down at her. His eyes looked very dark in the shade. Dark and mysterious. "The day she got here? No. I'd arranged to meet Cochburn on the mainland to order some supplies. She was already moved in by the time I got back."

"You said you saw her around, though. You must have talked to her at some point."

"Once or twice. Mostly we just said hello. I didn't see her out much. She seemed to enjoy her privacy."

"She didn't say anything at all about leaving the island?" Carrie pressed.

"No, but like I said, we barely spoke. I stay pretty busy around here. I don't have a lot of time to stop and shoot the breeze with the tenants."

And yet he'd taken the time to show her around the island today. Carrie couldn't help wondering about his motive.

"What about Ethan Stone? Have you seen much of him since he got here?"

Nick shrugged. "No. He pretty much stays holed up in his apartment."

Carrie remembered standing outside Stone's door the night before and the intense premonition of danger that had swept over her. And then she'd gone back to Tia's apartment and dreamed about a monster.

She suppressed a shiver as she glanced

up at Nick. "You don't find it strange that he never leaves his apartment?"

"Not particularly. Like I told you yesterday, people usually have a specific reason for coming to Cape Diablo. They're either running away or hiding out."

"And what about you?" Carrie blurted. "Which category do you fit into?"

Something flashed in his eyes, but he turned away before she could read him. "I came here to work."

"And that's the only reason?"

He turned back to face her, his gaze cold and steady once again. "Why all the questions? I've told you everything I know about your friend. If you think I had something to do with her leaving Cape Diablo—"

"I don't," Carrie said quickly. "It's not that."

"Then why the third degree?"

"I'm curious," she said, and then a little more reluctantly, "And I guess I'm in a strange mood today. Something happened last night that has me a little puzzled."

He frowned. "What?"

Carrie wasn't sure how much she wanted to tell him about her experience outside Ethan Stone's door. It sounded so bizarre, even to her. What if Nick thought she was crazy?

And what if she was? What if last night had been nothing more than her imagination playing tricks on her? What if the island was getting to her somehow?

She'd thought yesterday that Cape Diablo seemed like a living, breathing entity. Maybe it was. Maybe the island was capable of manipulating her emotions. Maybe it could even use her own fears and weaknesses against her.

And now she truly did sound insane, Carrie thought.

Besides, she'd experienced a premonition of danger before she ever arrived on Cape Diablo. She'd known Tia was in trouble the moment she read her letter.

"What happened last night?" Nick prompted.

Carrie gave a little shake of her head. "I don't even know how to explain it. At least not without sounding a little unhinged…" She paused. "After you came by, I went up to Ethan Stone's apartment. I heard him moving around, and I wanted to ask him if he'd seen Tia. But he wouldn't answer his door."

"Maybe he didn't hear you."

"No, I think he did hear me," Carrie said slowly. "Those apartments are small and I knocked loudly. The weird thing is…I had this feeling that he was right on the other side of the door. That he was…" She trailed off.

Nick flicked the twig away. When Carrie glanced at him he was watching her intently. "Go on."

"I had a feeling that if he opened the door, I'd be in terrible danger."

Instead of laughing at her, his frown deepened. "From Stone?"

She lifted one shoulder. "I don't know. I'm not sure if the danger I picked up on was coming from him or...something inside his apartment." She tucked a strand of hair behind one ear. "Believe me, I know how weird all this sounds, but it was like I knew something bad had happened in that apartment. Or was about to happen."

Nick said nothing, but she could tell that he was carefully weighing everything she'd told him. If he questioned her sanity, he kept his doubts hidden. "What did you do?"

She gave a shaky laugh. "Nothing heroic, I'm afraid. I ran down the steps and I would have retreated back inside Tia's apartment, but I saw Alma Garcia in the courtyard."

"And?"

"That was another odd thing." Carrie ran her hands up and down her arms, suddenly chilled. "She stood by the pool for the longest time, just gazing into the water. It was almost as if she was looking for something."

"She didn't say anything?"

"She didn't even see me," Carrie said.

"At least I don't think so. And then after a while, she turned, looked up at the loggia and…crossed herself. As if…"

"As if she felt what you'd felt."

"*Exactly.*"

The whole time she'd been talking, Nick's eyes never left hers. Carrie had never been the object of a more penetrating focus. It reminded her of the way he'd mesmerized her in her dream the night before. She was afraid he might be capable of doing that to her now so she tore her gaze away.

"Do you want me to talk to Stone?"

His tone more than the question took her by surprise. He sounded…concerned. Maybe even a bit protective and Carrie wasn't sure how she felt about that. She needed to fight her own battles because if she gave in to her fears even once, the demons and monsters would come rushing back into her life.

She'd put up a lot of barriers after the abduction. Safeguards to keep out the evil, but also to repel men like Nick Draco. Men who pushed her out of her comfort zone and made her feel vulnerable and overwhelmed. Carrie didn't like losing control, not in any aspect of her life. That was one of the reasons Tia's disappearance was so troubling to her. If Tia wasn't on Cape Diablo, Carrie had no idea what to do next.

"I appreciate the offer," she said a bit coolly. "But I'm probably just letting my imagination get the better of me. Besides, if I want to find out more about Ethan Stone, I'll go up and talk to him myself."

"Or maybe you should just leave well enough alone," Nick said. "You don't know anything about this guy. I told you earlier I'm not one for discounting intuition. If you're picking up bad vibes, my advice is to stay the hell away from him."

And what about the vibes I'm picking up from you?

Carrie's every instinct demanded that she pull back from Nick Draco, that she not give in to the temptation his steely eyes seemed to offer.

And yet she found herself thinking more and more about that dream. She couldn't get it out of her head. The vision of her and Nick together portended something dark and powerful in their attraction, as if they were dealing with forces neither of them could control.

A cold chill seeped over Carrie as their gazes connected and lingered. She knew what Nick was thinking at that moment. She could see it in his eyes. He wanted her, and she had a feeling that he was a man who always got what he wanted.

One way or another.

"ARE THE MOSQUITOES always this bad?" Carrie asked a little while later as they headed back up the path from the swamp.

"This is nothing." Nick glanced over his shoulder. "You should come down here sometime after the sun goes down. They get downright vicious after dark."

"Thanks for the warning." Carrie absently scratched a bite on the inside of her elbow. "What's that building over there?" She pointed to a weathered, clapboard structure that looked even more decrepit than the main house.

"Home sweet home," Nick said with the barest hint of a grin.

Carrie glanced at him in surprise. "You live there?"

"It's not as bad as it looks. My understanding is that it was originally built for the housekeeper and her family, but I don't think there's enough money in the trust for live-in help these days. Someone comes from the mainland every couple of weeks or so to do the heavy lifting."

Carrie's gaze drifted over the structure. Some of the shingles were missing from the roof, and the porch sagged so badly at one end, it seemed as if a good stiff wind might rip it off. But she assumed the building was sturdier than it looked.

Carrie wondered why Nick hadn't been given more suitable quarters in the main house. Surely there was plenty of room. Alma occupied the third floor and Carlos lived in the boathouse. The rest of the place stood empty except for the leased apartments.

"You don't mind living so close to the swamp? How do you stand all these bugs?" She tried to wave off a swarm that had vectored in on her head.

Nick shrugged. "It's not so bad. You get used to it. Besides, mosquitoes don't seem to like my blood. You, on the other hand…"

Carrie grimaced. "Tell me about it. I'm getting eaten alive out here." She slapped another one on her arm. "Yikes! We have mosquitoes in Miami, but nothing like this."

Nick gave her an amused looked as she continued to swat and scratch. "Come inside and I'll hook you up with some re-pellant."

"I've got some back at the apartment," Carrie said. "I bought a can before I left the marina yesterday. Besides, I really shouldn't take up any more of your time. I'm sure you need to get back to work."

"I don't exactly punch a time clock around here. I'll let you know when I need to get back."

"Fair enough," Carrie murmured. She followed him up the steps and waited while he fished a key from his pocket. At one time she might have wondered why he felt the need to lock the door on an island as tiny and secluded as Cape Diablo, but not anymore. Not after last night.

In spite of the row of windows across the front of the tiny house, the interior was cool and dim. Or maybe it just seemed that way after being out in the blazing sun. Whatever the case, Carrie paused inside the doorway, appreciating the reprieve.

"You can clean up in there." Nick

pointed to one of two doors off the main living area.

"Thanks."

Just like the rest of the house, the bathroom was tiny and sparse with the scent of the jungle permeating through the open window. A screen kept insects out, but the heat seeped through, making Carrie gaze longingly at the shower.

She was hot, tired and discouraged. They'd searched most of the island and found no sign of Tia anywhere. If she was still here, then where could she be? And if she really had left Cape Diablo, where on earth had she gone to?

Carrie stared at her reflection in the mirror as she quickly washed her hands. She hadn't put on any makeup that morning and had barely taken the time to brush her hair. She looked exhausted and felt it, but she didn't bother to try and make herself more presentable. Nick had already seen her at her worst.

And anyway, why should she care what he thought?

Drying her hands, she went back out to join him. He brought over two icy bottles of water from the refrigerator and handed one to her. "Have a seat."

She accepted the water gratefully and sat down at the rickety dining table. Nick went back into the kitchen for something, and as she watched him move about the tiny space, she thought about how easily he'd negotiated the sloping roof that morning. He was fully dressed now, but the image of his shirtless torso, burnished by the sun, suddenly seemed stuck on autoplay in her head.

She wanted to glance away before he caught her staring, but she couldn't seem to make her eyes oblige.

And then it was too late because he turned just then and their gazes met. A thrill traced down Carrie's spine, and she wondered if *he* could tell what *she* was thinking. She wanted him, too. Wanted him in a way that frightened her because Nick Draco was the kind of man who could devastate a woman if she wasn't careful.

"So what's next?" he asked as he pulled out the chair across from her and sat down.

For one breathless moment, Carrie thought he was talking about them, but then she came to her senses and realized what he meant. "I don't know. Since I'm stuck here until the supply boat comes on Friday, I have a couple of days to decide what to do next.

"I'm assuming you've already considered contacting Tia's family and friends to see if they've heard from her."

Carrie frowned. "That's not so easy. She doesn't have any family. She's an only child and her parents are dead. As for other friends…I'm not even sure she has anyone besides me."

He paused with the water bottle halfway to his lips. "What do you mean you're not sure? I thought the two of you were pretty tight."

"We are. Or at least…we were." Carrie traced a drop of condensation down the side of her bottle. "Maybe I gave you the wrong impression earlier. Tia and I aren't as close as we used to be. Until recently, we'd lost touch for a few years."

He looked as if he wanted to comment, but then he changed his mind and shrugged. "What about her work? She must have given some indication to her employer when she'd be back."

"I don't think she would have contacted anyone there," Carrie said. "She quit her job right before her wedding."

That stopped him again. "She's married?"

"Actually, she called off the ceremony right before she came out here," Carrie said. "She left a note at the church saying that she couldn't go through with the marriage."

He grimaced. "That's pretty cold."

"If you knew her fiancé, you'd understand why she wouldn't want to face him."

Carrie bit her lip. "In fact, I think he's the reason she picked Cape Diablo. She was probably hoping he wouldn't be able to find her here."

"Why? Was he abusive?" Suddenly Nick's voice was as cold as his eyes.

"I don't have any proof. But I'd say he definitely has violent tendencies. I only met him a few times, but I sensed something wasn't right from the first. He seemed too perfect, like those men you see on the news who strangle their wives and dump their bodies at sea. I'm not suggesting he did anything like that," Carrie said quickly. "But I do think Tia may have seen something in him before the wedding that scared her. He has a pretty explosive temper. I found that out the hard way."

Nick's gaze sharpened. "What do you mean? Did he do something to you?"

"Not physically, no. But I'm the one who broke the news to him that Tia had left him at the altar. Needless to say, he didn't take it well. If we'd been alone, I'm not sure what he would have done."

Nick's expression never altered, but Carrie could tell that he didn't like what he was hearing. Although he certainly had no reason to feel protective of her. The two of them were virtual strangers. "You think he somehow found out that she was here?"

"The thought has crossed my mind," Carrie said.

Nick studied her for a moment. "And you came here to what? Rescue her?"

"I just came here to make sure she was okay," Carrie said a bit defensively.

Something flickered in his eyes that she couldn't define. "How did you know where to find her?"

"She mentioned the name of the island in her letter and I did a Google search. A few phone calls led me to Robert Cochburn."

"You said earlier that it wasn't just the letter, but her tone that concerned you," Nick mused. "Did she sound scared, desperate…what? Did she say anything that made you think her jilted fiancé had threatened her?"

"She didn't say anything about Trey at all. It was almost as if she'd already put him out of her mind. She mainly wrote about Cape Diablo and the Santiago family. I even found copies of newspaper articles in her apartment that she printed off the Internet. Which is why I can't help wondering…" Carrie paused. "Do you think it's possible she could have uncovered something about the family's disappearance that put her in danger?"

"I doubt it. The only two people still alive connected to the Santiagos are Alma and Carlos. They're both pretty eccentric, but I don't think they're violent."

Carrie nodded. "You're probably right. I'm grasping at straws. I still can't understand how Tia could have left the island without anyone seeing her. It makes me wonder how long it would have taken for anyone to miss her if I hadn't shown up asking questions."

"So what about you?" Nick asked slowly. "You're stranded here until Friday. Is someone going to come look for you?"

Why was he asking? Carrie wondered anxiously. Personal curiosity or something else? "I left my itinerary at work," she lied.

He half smiled as if he knew she'd thought that one up on the spur of the moment. "What is it that you do?"

"I'm a graphic designer. I work for a local magazine in Miami. Basically, I'm a visual problem solver." She stood abruptly, not wanting to answer any more questions about her private life. "I appreciate your showing me around the island this morning, but I should get going. I didn't mean to take up so much of your time."

"You didn't. I wanted to help you search." He walked her to the front door and out on the porch, although Carrie would have preferred that he didn't. Suddenly, she was anxious to get away from him. All she wanted at the moment was to get back to the safe little life she'd created for herself in Miami. The sooner she left Cape Diablo and Nick Draco behind, the better for her peace of mind.

He propped one hand on the newel post as he stared down at her. "At least now you know that Tia isn't still on the island."

That was little comfort. Because if Tia wasn't on Cape Diablo, then someone else had left the friendship pendant on her bedroom floor. Someone else had gone to a great deal of trouble to try and keep Carrie on the island.

She thought again of the man in the newspaper article—Adam Pritchard—and shuddered. Were he and Nathaniel Glover one and the same?

A lengthy incarceration would certainly explain why he hadn't tried to come back for her as the profiler had predicted that he would.

What if Glover had been the one to leave the pendant on Tia's bedroom floor?

What if he'd used Tia to lure Carrie to

the island? What if he'd found a new lair and he had Tia there now?

She and Nick had searched most of Cape Diablo, but there were dozens of other islands only a short boat ride away. He might have Tia on one of those now.

Or was he hiding somewhere in plain sight?

She thought again of the danger she'd sensed outside Ethan Stone's door the night before. Was it possible—

"Are you sure you're okay?" Nick's anxious question cut into her thoughts. "You look a little green around the gills. You didn't get too much sun, did you?"

Carrie shook her head, trying to dispel her wild ramblings. Nathaniel Glover— or whatever his name was—couldn't be anywhere near Cape Diablo. He had nothing to do with Tia's absence. It was too far-fetched to believe otherwise. "I'm fine. Just concerned about Tia."

"She'll turn up." Nick nodded in the direction of the main house. "Don't veer too far off the path. It'll take you straight back to the courtyard."

Don't veer too far off the path.

If only she never had, Carrie thought.

Chapter Eight

Nick watched from the porch until Carrie was out of sight, then he turned and went back inside the house. Retrieving his laptop from a locked briefcase, he established a satellite linkup and shot off an e-mail to headquarters requesting information on both Carrie Bishop and Tia Falcon. Then he typed each of their names into a search engine and scrolled through the links.

Alone, their names didn't generate anything out of the ordinary, but when he typed the two together, he was linked to an old article on a Web site for missing and exploited children.

Quickly, he scanned the text.

The two girls had been abducted after sneaking off the grounds of the summer camp they were attending. The authorities were notified when they didn't show up for dinner, and within hours, a full-scale manhunt had been launched.

One of the girls was found the next day wandering down a rural road two hundred miles from where she'd been grabbed. She was taken to an area hospital and treated for minor injuries while the police and FBI were called in.

Later, she was able to give the authorities a thorough description of her abductor and the van he'd driven.

She was also able to lead them back to the remote cabin in the woods where he had held her and her friend hostage. The suspect had already fled with the other girl, and it wasn't until almost a week later that an anonymous tip had led the FBI to a motel where they found twelve-year-old Tia Falcon bound and gagged in one of the rooms.

The kidnapper was never apprehended.

So that was it, Nick thought as he logged off and put away the computer.

That was the demon that still haunted Carrie Bishop. That was why she was so desperate to find Tia. Why she still felt responsible for her friend's well-being.

Carrie had managed to escape their abductor, but Tia hadn't.

Now it all made sense...Carrie's almost obsessive desperation and her willingness to put herself at risk for the sake of finding her friend.

It was a classic case of survivor's guilt.

Nick had seen it before, in others...and in himself.

As CARRIE STEPPED through the gate into the courtyard, her gaze went immediately to the loggia over Tia's apartment. She peered into the shadows, waiting to experience that same sense of danger that had scared her so badly the night before.

In the light of day, all she felt was a

vague uneasiness. Maybe she *had* let her imagination get the better of her. Maybe Ethan Stone was exactly who Cochburn said he was—a burned-out executive desperately in need of some downtime.

But even if her imagination had run wild on the loggia, she hadn't imagined Alma Garcia's odd behavior by the pool.

Slowly, Carrie walked over and stared into the murky water. What had the woman been looking for?

Carrie could barely see the bottom through the accumulation of leaves and algae. The pool had been badly neglected for months, perhaps years, and she wondered why Cochburn didn't have it drained. Maybe Alma wouldn't let him.

On impulse, Carrie snapped a few shots of the pool, then her gaze lifted to the back of the main house and she wondered if Alma was up there now watching from the shadows of her room. She was a strange woman. Demented, according to Cochburn, from her years of isolation on Cape Diablo.

Was it possible that she knew something regarding Tia's whereabouts?

Cochburn had said she wasn't lucid enough to make much sense when he'd spoken to her yesterday, but Carrie had no way of knowing how hard he'd even tried. Perhaps he'd only pretended to speak to Alma to appease her.

He also said that Alma rarely left her third-floor quarters, but she'd been out and about last night. Maybe the woman wasn't quite as demented—or housebound—as the attorney had let on.

Would Alma talk to her? Carrie wondered.

Maybe after all these years of isolation, she might enjoy some afternoon company. Besides, all she could do was say no.

Turning away from the pool, Carrie walked over to a set of French doors that opened from the back of the house into the courtyard. She tried the latch and found that it was unlocked. Glancing over her shoulder, she quickly stepped inside.

Cochburn had mentioned nothing about rules or regulations regarding the mansion. If the main house was off-limits to the tenants, he surely would have said something. After all, he'd made a point to warn her about the swamp.

But Carrie still felt as if she were trespassing as she paused inside the door and glanced around.

The interior of the house was dim and cool. The walls were stucco, the floors a dark red Mexican tile. Carrie found herself in a long, wide hallway that led, she presumed, to the front of the house.

She followed it all the way to the foyer and to a wide, curving staircase trimmed with an intricate wrought iron banister.

All the way down the hallway, Carrie kept glancing over her shoulder. The house was so quiet, almost like a tomb. Through open doorways, she glimpsed high-ceilinged rooms and furniture covered with sheets. She tried to imagine how it must have been in its heyday with the doors and windows thrown open to the breezes and the sound of children's laughter drifting up from the beach.

And then one night, Alma and Carlos had returned from a celebration on the mainland to find that the family had vanished. The blood in the boathouse where Carlos now lived was the only clue that violence had been done, but the bodies had never been found.

Carrie preferred to think that Andres had packed up his family and fled in the middle of the night, perhaps one step ahead of the law or a brutal enemy. She wanted to believe that they'd landed somewhere safe and sound, and that the girls—grown now—were leading happy, normal lives.

But as she made her way up the creaking stairs, a dark oppression settled over her. Somehow she didn't think the Santiagos had had a happy ending. The house seemed secretive, brooding, as if memories of something evil were trapped inside the walls.

At the top of the stairs, another long hallway opened before her. At the end, she could see the stairway to the third story, but Carrie lingered on the second floor, reluctant to disturb Alma Garcia. She couldn't help remembering Robert Cochburn's description of her. *"She's harmless. Crazy as a bat, but harmless."*

Her behavior the night before certainly seemed eccentric, to say the least, but Carrie could only imagine what her own frame of mind would be like after thirty years of isolation on Cape Diablo.

As she made her way down the hallway toward the staircase, she tried a few of the doors. Most of them were locked, but she found an open one near the end of the corridor and glancing over her shoulder, slipped inside.

She'd hoped it would turn out to be the children's bedroom. Tia had seemed so obsessed with the little girls in her letter that Carrie was curious to learn more about them. Obviously, Tia felt a kinship with the children and Carrie still wondered, despite Nick's doubts, if perhaps she had stumbled across something about the missing family that had put her own life in jeopardy.

But rather than being a child's bedroom, the area appeared to be used for storage. Boxes, trunks and discarded furniture had been piled into the space in a haphazard fashion.

Taking another quick glance down the hallway, Carrie closed the door softly behind her and stood gazing around. Dust motes danced in a beam of light from the window and cobwebs glistened in shadowy corners. On first glance it appeared as if no one had been in the room for years, but then she noticed the telltale footprints on the dusty wood floor and evidence that some of the boxes and trunks had recently been rearranged.

Had Tia been up here? Had she gone through the old boxes and trunks looking for clues about the missing children?

Had someone caught her in here?

Carrie shivered as she threw another glance toward the door. Maybe she shouldn't be in here, either. She thought again of Alma Garcia's strange behavior by the pool and the muffled voices she'd heard on the other side of the wall. Who had she gone to meet outside last night?

Something strange was going on here. Something Carrie didn't yet understand, but whatever it was, she had a bad feeling that Tia had ended up in the middle of it.

Kneeling, she blew a film of dust off one of the trunks and opened the lid to have a quick peek inside. The smell of moth balls drifted up from the hodgepodge of clothing and toys. Someone—probably Alma—must have put away the little girls' things after they were gone.

But as Carrie sifted through the items, she realized that the clothing and toys had belonged to a little boy. The T-shirts and shorts were unmistakably masculine, as were the tiny toy soldiers and plastic boats.

Who had these things belonged to? she

wondered. Cochburn had said nothing about Andres Santiago having a son. Neither had Tia. She'd only talked about Reyna and Pilar.

Had Alma Garcia had a child?

A worn Teddy bear had been stuffed in the bottom of the trunk, and as Carrie pulled it out, a chill descended over her. She glanced quickly over her shoulder to see if someone had come up behind her. No one was there, of course, but the feeling of being watched was so strong that her heart started to pound in fear.

Quickly she placed the bear back in the trunk and closed the lid. The feeling dissipated, but Carrie was still unnerved. She wanted to leave the room, but for a reason she couldn't explain, she walked over to the window and glanced out.

Beyond the stucco wall, the crystalline waters of the Gulf shimmered in the blazing sun, but her attention was caught not by the glorious view, but by a movement below in the courtyard. It took her a moment to pick out the man from the shadows, and she thought at first it might be Nick. But as he trudged out of the shade into the full sunlight, she saw that the man was much older. His stooped shoulders and shambling gait made him seem ancient.

He stood at the side of the pool, gazing into the murky depths much as Alma had done the night before. He seemed transfixed by something, and Carrie wondered what he and Alma found so fascinating about the water.

And then she saw it. It was only a flash. A brief glimpse of something small and dark floating beneath the surface. A shadow, maybe, or...

A body.

Carrie's heart slammed against her chest. It was just a shadow, she tried to tell herself. She'd been fooled before by the murky water. It was just a shadow.

A shadow that seemed to disappear before her eyes.

Carrie blinked. It had been there one moment and now it was gone.

Slowly the old man turned and his gaze lifted to the window where she stood...almost as if he'd known all along that she was there.

A fishing hat was pulled low over his face, shading his eyes, but even from that distance, Carrie could tell that his skin was leathered and creased from years of working under the hot sun.

Something about the way he stared up at her, the way his dark eyes seemed to pierce right through the glass, caused her to step back from the window with a gasp.

When she glanced back, he was gone, too.

Carrie had no idea how he could have disappeared so quickly. When she'd first seen him, his movements had seemed labored and deliberate, almost as if he were in pain, but in the space of a few seconds he'd vanished just like the shadow in the pool.

She tried to tell herself that he'd merely

stepped back into the shade of the house where she couldn't see him. She didn't believe in ghosts even though she'd been haunted by her past for years. Besides, she knew who the man was even though she'd never set eyes on him before. He was Carlos Lazario, the caretaker.

If she ran downstairs, she might be able to catch up with him and ask him about Tia. She hurried over to the door, but as she drew it open, the squeak of floorboards in the hallway halted her.

Carlos?

She didn't think he would have had time to get inside and up the stairs. Not unless he knew a secret passageway. Carrie thought about the way he'd stared up at her, and nerves fluttered in her stomach.

Trying to calm her racing heart, she glanced out into the hallway. When she saw Alma Garcia, she quickly stepped back from the door.

Carrie waited until she was sure Alma had passed by the storeroom before glancing out again. She saw Alma pause in front of the room at the top of the stairs and bend to set a wicker laundry basket on the floor. Then she unlocked the door and disappeared inside.

Carrie had no idea what the woman was doing. If she was cleaning the room, she might be inside for a while and Carrie had no desire to be trapped in the dusty storeroom for the rest of the afternoon. Slipping into the hallway, she quietly closed the door behind her, then tiptoed down the corridor.

Alma had left the door slightly ajar, and Carrie could hear her talking to someone inside. Carrie hesitated just outside. Who was in there with Alma? And why had the door been locked?

Could Tia be inside?

Carrie placed a hand on the door, intent on shoving it open and confronting Alma Garcia, but then she froze as the woman's voice rose in irritation.

"Stop hiding from me! I'm warning you both. I'm in no mood for games."

A pause. Then, "If you aren't out here by the time I count to ten, I'll have to tell your father how naughty you've been. You don't want that, do you? No, I didn't think so. Now come out at once!"

Carrie didn't know whether to be relieved or even more alarmed. Alma Garcia was inside that room scolding two little girls who had been missing for over thirty years. Her dementia was even worse than Robert Cochburn had indicated. He had said she wasn't dangerous, but obviously he didn't know the full extent of her condition.

"All right, have it your way," she said with a resigned sigh. "But when I find you..." Her voice trailed off on an implied threat.

Carrie hurried back to the storeroom and slipped inside. Watching from a crack in the door, she saw Alma leave the room, gather up the basket and continue down the hallway, stopping at each door to look inside. A few minutes later she disappeared down the stairs.

Slipping from her hiding place, Carrie followed at a discreet distance. When she reached the bottom of the stairs, she hung back, not wanting Alma to spot her. But she needn't have worried. The older woman seemed oblivious to anything but her fruitless search.

Carrie had almost decided to leave Alma to the hunt when she saw the woman open a door and descend another set of stairs. Carrie wondered if the steps led down to some sort of wine cellar. She wanted to investigate the space herself, but knew that she would have to wait until Alma left.

It didn't take long. The woman appeared a few moments later, and Carrie waited until she was out of sight, then she glided silently across the tile floor and tried the door. It opened on well-oiled hinges and Carrie stood at the top of the steps, looking down into a dark abyss. She felt for a light switch and flipped it. A bare light bulb was the only illumination, so Carrie moved cautiously as she made her way down the steps.

At the bottom of the stairs was another door, this one locked tight. Carrie couldn't budge it. She put her ear to the thick wood, but she could hear nothing inside.

"Tia?" she whispered. "Are you down here?"

The only answer that came was the stealthy scurry of something in the shadows.

Rats, Carrie thought with a shiver. She remembered the smell in Tia's apartment the day before, and wondered if this was how the rodents were getting inside the house.

Going back up the stairs, she turned off the light and closed the door behind her. Then making sure the coast was clear, she hurried from the house, suddenly anxious to be out in the sunshine.

THAT NIGHT CARRIE stood at the window and watched flashes of lightning in the west. Another storm was moving in from the Gulf, and she wondered how soon it would hit. Not that it mattered. Bad weather was the least of her worries.

Her gaze lifted to the back of the mansion. Something flickered briefly in the glass, but she couldn't tell if it was reflected lightning or if someone was up there moving about.

Carrie thought instantly of Alma Garcia and the way she'd gone through the house looking for the missing children. She'd seemed oblivious to everything else almost as if she'd been sleepwalking, but Carrie didn't think that was the case. The woman lived inside her own little world. A world that had stopped turning for her over thirty years ago.

But was her self-imposed exile from civilization the sole cause of her dementia or could the island itself be to blame?

The notion struck Carrie suddenly and she shivered.

Could a place be evil?

Could violent emotions linger for so long that they somehow became a presence?

Carrie had sensed something strange from the moment she first set foot on the island. She'd experienced the same sensation in that terrible little cabin in the woods fourteen years ago. She didn't know if the evil was real or her own imagination, but she was suddenly very frightened.

Rubbing her hands up and down her arms, she tried to rationalize her fears. If violence had been done on Cape Diablo, perhaps the lingering vibes were from the demise of the Santiago family. Her premonitions of danger might have nothing to do with the present, but as the storm drew near, her unease deepened.

Tia's letter.

The strange phone call that had come in the middle of the night.

The friendship pendant that had been left on the floor for her to find.

Someone had laid a very clever trail for

her to follow, and that trail had brought her to Cape Diablo.

Carrie could think of only one person who would be obsessed enough to use her guilt against her.

Her recklessness had caused her and Tia to leave the campgrounds that day, and her guilt had kept her from succumbing to the terror of their situation. She'd wanted desperately to rescue Tia because it was the only way that she could redeem herself.

But instead, she'd saved herself and left Tia in the clutches of a monster more frightening and dangerous than anything either of their imaginations could have conjured.

She doubted that Tia had ever been able to forgive her, because Carrie certainly couldn't forgive herself.

As she watched the lightning, her mind drifted back in time. She didn't want to think about the past, but on Cape Diablo, the memories had grown too strong to resist....

THE SCREAMS HAD FINALLY stopped, but the silence was even more terrifying. Carrie tried not to think about the unnatural quiet and what it might mean. Tia was still alive. She had to be. And Carrie would find a way to save them both.

But Tia had been gone for a long time. Hours and hours. Their captor would be back soon. For Carrie.

She shivered uncontrollably thinking about what he might do to her. What he had already done to Tia. It must have been something awful. Something...unspeakable. Tia's screams were like nothing Carrie had ever heard before. They hadn't even sounded human.

But now Carrie longed for those screams because the quiet meant...

No, she wouldn't think about that.

She wouldn't let herself think about anything but finding a way out.

But she'd been over their tiny prison a dozen times, and had almost given up hope when she discovered something at the window.

The metal grid covering the opening was bolted into the wall on all four sides, but near the bottom left corner, one of the screws had worked loose in the rotting wood. Carrie still couldn't twist it with her fingers, though, and the only tool she could find was the edge of the friendship pendant she wore around her neck. The metal was thin and frail and she had to be very careful not to bend or break the heart as she worked at the screw.

It took her a long time and when she was finished, her fingers were numb from where she'd gripped the edge of the heart. She slipped her hands up under the grid and tried to work it loose, but the other screws held it in place. She would have to remove the others, but that could take hours and she instinctively knew she didn't have much time.

Crossing the floor, she pressed her ear to the door and listened. She could hear nothing. She had no idea if Tia was even still inside the cabin. Maybe he'd taken her out into the woods and…

Don't think about that!

Carrie hurried back over to the window and started working on the second fastener. This one took even longer because it was still screwed tightly into the wood.

After a while, Carrie began to worry that she might never be able to loosen it, but she kept at it until she felt it give slightly. A little more pressure…another turn…and she finally had it free.

Once again she tried putting her hands underneath the bottom of the grid and tugging it away from the wall, but the opening between the metal and the window was still not large enough for her to slip through.

By now hours must have passed. Carrie had no idea how long they'd been in the cabin or how long Tia had been gone. Her stomach growled for food and her muscles ached from remaining in one position for so long. But she wouldn't give up. She couldn't.

The third screw finally free, Carrie slipped the chain around her neck, then gave the grid another yank. The bottom gave way from the wall just enough so that she could squeeze up under it. Then she could pull herself up to the windowsill.

But first she would wait for their abductor to bring Tia back. Carrie couldn't leave without her. They were in this together.

Crawling over to the mattress, she lay down facing the window. Maybe if she pretended to sleep, he would leave her alone when he came back. Then she and Tia could climb out the window and somehow they'd find their way back to camp. Or to a road. Somewhere, anywhere, far far away from this awful place.

Carrie heard footsteps approaching the door and a split second before his key slipped into the lock, she realized her plan would never work. The grid was pulled out from the wall. He'd see it the moment he opened the door. He'd bolt it back in place or take Tia and Carrie somewhere else and they'd never get away from him then.

Carrie's heart was pounding so hard she could barely breathe. Scrambling to the window, she slid her body underneath the metal and as she pulled herself up to the sill, her shirt caught on the jagged edge of the grid. She tugged and tugged, but she couldn't get it free.

And then the door opened and the man stepped inside.

He saw her at the window and screamed in rage as he lunged for her.

Frantically, Carrie yanked at the tail of her shirt until the fabric finally ripped away. But it had cost her precious seconds. As she balanced herself on the sill, he reached under the grid and clamped a hand around her arm.

Carrie fought him, but his grip was too strong. He held her with one hand while with the other he tried to rip the grid from the wall so that he could get at her. Instinctively, Carrie lashed out at him, digging her nails deeply into his flesh.

The pain seemed to infuriate him even more. He released her then so that he could tear at the grid with both hands, and Carrie went tumbling to the ground.

She landed with a bone-jarring thud on her stomach, and for a moment, she lay with the wind knocked out of her, too dazed and frightened to move. Then she came to her senses and jumped to her feet.

Which way?

All around her was darkness. Carrie had no idea where she was, which way she should go....

Behind her, she heard him curse and then he went completely silent. For one split second, hope flooded through Carrie. If he couldn't get the grid off the window, he wouldn't be able to follow her. If she could somehow find Tia...

He came out the front door at a run.

Carrie heard his footsteps pound across the porch and down the steps, and she knew that she had to run or find a hiding place....

He came around the corner, saw her and stopped dead still.

From inside the cabin, Carrie heard a tiny noise. A whimper of pain...

She looked up and glimpsed someone standing at the window, watching her.

Tia! She was still alive!

And then the man laughed and started toward her....

THE MEMORY SKITTERED away as Carrie gasped. In a flash of lightning, she saw someone dart furtively across the courtyard. A woman...

Pressing closer to the window, Carrie peered into the darkness thinking it must be Alma Garcia. She was certainly eccentric enough to be out in a storm.

But as the woman reached the gate, another flicker of lightning drew her gaze skyward and for a split second, she stood highlighted against the dark backdrop of the jungle. Carrie's breath caught in recognition.

It was Tia.

Chapter Nine

Carrie's heart flailed against her chest as she threw open the door and screamed Tia's name. But it was too late. She'd already fled through the gate.

Carrie whirled and ran back inside. Grabbing a flashlight from the desk, she sprinted out the door and across the courtyard.

The storm had moved inland by now, and the lightning was so steady that she could see her way quite clearly. She shouldn't have wasted those precious seconds retrieving the flashlight, because in that brief time, Tia had vanished.

Carrie tried calling out to her, but the

wind had picked up and her voice was lost in the thrashing of leaves overhead.

Had it really been Tia? Carrie wondered desperately. Or had her mind conjured her friend's face? She'd been so lost in thought, so caught up in the past that it was entirely possible she'd imagined the whole thing.

But she wouldn't give up searching. Not yet. What if it *had* been Tia?

She didn't stop until the trail split, and then she paused to recall what Nick had told her earlier. If she stayed on the path it would take her into the swamp. Veering right would lead her to the harbor.

Carrie had no idea which way Tia had gone. She wasn't even sure that it was Tia she was chasing. She wondered if, like Alma Garcia, she was becoming demented, delusional. If Tia had been in the courtyard, why wouldn't she have come to her? Why had she run away when Carrie called her name?

Nothing made sense on this island.

Carrie stood indecisively, not knowing which way to go. Then a voice drifted up from the water and she hurried toward the sound.

She came out of the trees on a slight incline that overlooked the harbor. Two boats—one motorboat and a larger fishing vessel—were anchored side by side and she could see men moving about in the stormy darkness, their voices rising over the wind and the crashing waves.

The boats bounced and strained against their moorings, and Carrie wondered what had brought the men out in such weather.

Instinctively, she knew that she shouldn't let them see her, but just as she turned back to the path, a hand clapped over her mouth as an arm wrapped around her waist and dragged her back into the trees.

She would have fought him, but she recognized him almost instantly. Nick put his lips against her ear and said, "Be quiet. Those men have guns. If they hear us, they'll shoot us, understand?"

She nodded.

He eased his hand away, but he didn't release her. One arm still held her just below her breasts while the other hand rested at her throat.

Carrie's heart beat a wild staccato against her chest. In fear, yes, but also because of Nick's closeness. Because of the way he held her...

They stood that way for the longest time watching the boats, and once, when Nick shifted his weight, his arm grazed the underside of her breasts. Desire shot through her, so quick and hot she almost gasped out loud.

At that moment, Carrie wasn't certain who she feared more. Nick...or the armed men in the boats.

Their nefarious business concluded, the men parted ways. The small boat took off first and was soon lost among the swells. The larger vessel was slower and more stable on the choppy seas, but it, too, was running without lights. Carrie thought both drivers must be out of their minds to be out in such weather.

She glanced up, saw the hard lines of Nick's face in the lightning and started to tremble.

"It's okay," he said, mistaking her reaction. "They're gone now. You're safe."

He released her and Carrie turned slowly to face him. "Who were those men?"

"Drug smugglers, most likely."

Her brows shot up. "Drug smugglers?"

"Don't sound so surprised," he said with a shrug. "This is Cape Diablo, after all."

Yes, and they'd just been talking about Andres Santiago's smuggling operation that very afternoon. "It's still shocking to see it in your own backyard," Carrie murmured. "What should we do?"

Now it was Nick's turn to sound surprised. "Do? I don't know about you, but I intend to keep my mouth shut," he said grimly.

"But...we have to tell the police, don't we?"

"Think about what you're saying,

Carrie." It was the first time he'd used her name, and Carrie felt a little thrill charge through her veins.

I must be crazy, she thought. Here they stood talking about drug dealers and all she could think about was the way Nick's voice sounded when he said her name. The way the lightning flashed over his face, making him seem more dangerous and exciting than ever.

"By the time we can get word to the mainland, those boats could be halfway back to South America," he said. "Then again, they could be holed up just an island or two away. If the police come snooping around Cape Diablo, they'll know someone talked. They could come back, and next time they might not leave any witnesses."

Carrie shivered. She put her hand on his arm, then dropped it quickly. "What if Tia saw those men? What if they know she can identify them?"

"That's not likely. I've been here three

weeks and that's the first time I've seen boats in the harbor."

"But I saw her in the courtyard earlier and it looked as if she was running away from someone," Carrie said desperately.

"You *what?*"

She nodded. "I saw her. At least…I think it was Tia. She ran through the gate and I followed her down here."

"You followed her down here to the harbor."

His voice sounded doubtful and Carrie frowned. "You don't believe me, do you?"

"You obviously believe you saw her. Are you sure it was Tia?"

Carrie hesitated. She'd been certain earlier, but now, in the face of Nick's skepticism, she was starting to have her own doubts. Maybe she'd seen Tia because she wanted to see Tia.

"Are you sure it wasn't Alma Garcia?" he pressed.

"I guess it could have been." And it made sense, considering that Carrie had seen Alma in the courtyard just the night before.

"Cochburn told me that she rarely leaves her apartment," Carrie muttered.

"Cochburn doesn't know what he's talking about." Nick's scorn for the attorney was apparent.

"But he was so helpful and concerned when I called about Tia," Carrie said. "And he came all the way out here with me yesterday to make sure I found the right island."

"Good for him. But if I were you, I'd think twice before putting my trust in a man I hardly know."

Was he warning her about Cochburn… or himself?

"Come on," he said, taking her arm. "Let's head back before the rain starts."

As they hurried back down the path, Carrie couldn't get his warning out of her head. She wanted to believe that she could trust Nick, but she didn't know anything about him. He was a stranger, and yet she found herself drawn to him in a way that left her breathless.

She'd had boyfriends before. She'd even had a few lovers. But no one had ever swept her off her feet the way Nick had.

When they emerged from the trees near his place, Carrie turned. "You don't have to come with me. I know my way back. And don't worry. I won't veer too far off the path," she said, repeating his earlier warning.

Although maybe she already had. Maybe she just didn't know it, yet.

BY THE TIME they made it back to the courtyard, the rain arrived. They hurried beneath the loggia and stood watching the downpour in silence.

Nick could see Carrie shivering in her wet clothing. In the rapid flashes of lightning, the outline of her bra showed plainly through the wet fabric of her T-shirt, but he didn't want to stare so he tore his gaze away.

She rubbed a hand up and down her arm. "I should probably go in."

"Yeah. That might be a good idea," he agreed. Although he wished she wouldn't.

"Do you want to come in and dry off?" she offered hesitantly.

"I'll just get wet again." He propped a hand on one of the support columns and stared down at her.

She seemed to grow flustered. "Why are you doing that?"

"What?"

"Looking at me that way."

"You know why," he murmured.

He heard the sharp intake of her breath and then turning her face up to his, she said in resignation, "Why don't you just kiss me and get it over with?"

"Now that's what I call an irresistible invitation," he said dryly.

She shrugged. "I didn't mean to offend you. It's just…I'm no good at this. I figured the sooner you knew, the sooner you'll—"

"The sooner I'll what?"

"Stop looking at me that way."

"I'm not the only one looking," he said softly.

"I know. I'm sorry." She bit her lip. "I shouldn't be leading you on."

"Is that what you're doing?"

"I'm attracted to you," she admitted reluctantly.

"Then what's the problem?" He leaned in so close their lips were almost touching.

"I'm not a good kisser," she warned.

"Why don't you let me be the judge of that?" He cupped a hand around the back of her neck and pulled her toward him.

He didn't touch her anywhere else nor did he kiss her at first. He merely stared down at her for the longest moment until he saw her lips tremble and part.

And then he lowered his head and gently traced the outline of her mouth with his tongue.

She gasped and drew back, but only for an instant. And then her mouth opened even more and he slipped his tongue inside.

He could tell she was inexperienced, but she was wrong about being a bad kisser. What she lacked in technique, she made up for in passion. As her tongue tangled with his, she put a hand on his chest and twisted her fingers in his shirt, tugging him closer, eagerly letting him know that she wanted more.

But he still didn't touch her, though God knows he wanted to. His hands itched to slide beneath her wet top and caress her full, round breasts. To hold her against him and let her feel how much he wanted her, too.

It was all he could do not to scoop her up and carry her inside to the bedroom, but Carrie Bishop was not a woman he wanted to take lightly. She'd been through a horror that few people could imagine, and the demons of her past still haunted her. He didn't want to give her yet another reason to retreat behind her walls.

When he finally broke the kiss, she leaned in, then caught herself and quickly stepped back. She touched her fingertips to her lips as she gazed up at him.

"How was I?"

He shrugged. "Not bad for a first kiss."

"That wasn't my first kiss," she said in a rush. "I may not have a lot of experience, but I've certainly been kissed before."

"I meant *our* first kiss," he said. "It was good, but the second is always better."

"I'll keep that in mind." Then she said almost shyly, "Now do you want to come in?"

He shook his head regretfully. "Not tonight. I need to get back down to the harbor and make sure those boats don't come back."

"But what if they do?" Her expression turned anxious. "Those men were armed."

"Don't worry. I'll be careful."

And he always had been…until tonight.

AS I WATCHED THEM from above, I knew that I was taking a risk. If they looked up, they would see me in the flashes of lightning, but I needn't have worried. They were oblivious to everything but each other. Completely impervious to the danger that lurked so near them...

The way he touched and kissed her made me burn with rage, but it wouldn't be long now. Soon it would happen. Soon I would let her see me, and all those hours of lonely solitude would melt away in that first moment of realization.

At long last, her time had come. I had saved the best for last.

But I couldn't let anticipation make me careless. I still had things to do.

I needed to get rid of the body because the smell would soon be overpowering.

Taking one last look, I slowly drifted back into the shadows.

Chapter Ten

Carrie awoke to sunlight streaming in through the bedroom window and someone banging on the front door. Alarmed by the sound, she swung her legs over the side of the bed and reached for her robe, pulling it on as she hurried down the hallway to the living room.

She'd left the blinds up last night, and she could see Nick standing outside the door as she approached. She had the strongest urge to touch her fingertips to her lips, as if she could still feel the heat of his kiss, but instead she shrugged off the memory and opened the door.

"Is something wrong?" she asked anxiously.

His gaze traveled over her, making those memories come back in full force. "Sorry to disturb you so early, but I wanted to let you know that the supply boat is here."

Carrie frowned. "But it's not supposed to be here until tomorrow."

Nick nodded. "Apparently, there's been a last-minute schedule change. Trawick's having engine problems and he got his cousin to cover for him. I guess this was the only day the new guy could make the run. Anyway, I thought you'd want to know because if you don't catch a ride today, you'll be stuck here until next Tuesday.

"But I'm not ready," Carrie protested. "I'm not even dressed yet."

His gaze moved over her again, more deliberate this time. More intimate. "Take your time. I'll go down and make sure he holds the boat for you."

Carrie folded her arms across the front of her robe, suddenly self-conscious under his relentless gaze. "What about Tia? What if it really was her I saw in the courtyard last night?"

"We searched the island," he said. "If she was here and wanted to be found, we would have found her."

"But it might not be that simple." Carrie raked a hand through her hair. "If she's in some sort of trouble, I don't want to leave without making sure she's okay. If something happens to her and I haven't done everything in my power to find her, I'd never be able to live with myself."

"I repeat, you can't find someone who doesn't want to be found," he said impatiently. Then his gaze softened as he stared down at her. Or perhaps that was her imagination, too, Carrie thought. "Look, I understand how you feel. But you've done all you can here. Maybe it's time to go home and regroup."

Carrie drew a long breath. He was right

and she knew it. She'd done all she could here. Besides, the longer she stayed on Cape Diablo, the greater the danger to herself.

She had feelings for Nick Draco, and if she hung around much longer, she just might get in over her head.

IT TOOK HER LESS THAN five minutes to pack. She'd only brought a few things with her, and after a second run-through of the apartment to make sure she hadn't left anything behind, she was ready to go.

Since she didn't have a current photo of Tia with her should she decide to go to the police, she took the engagement clipping from the desk in the living room and slipped it into her bag.

Letting herself out of the apartment, Carrie pocketed the spare key. She'd have to mail it to Robert Cochburn as soon as she got home. Somehow it didn't seem right leaving it in Tia's apartment even though the door had been left unlocked when Carrie first came. Still, she didn't want to take a chance that someone else could wander inside and go through Tia's personal belongings. Carrie knew how much she would hate that.

She surveyed the courtyard, her gaze moving from the murky pool, upward to the third-story windows and finally to the upstairs apartment. Everything about the place was creepy and oppressive, and she couldn't deny that a part of her was relieved to be leaving. Here on Cape Diablo, the nightmares had found her again, and Carrie had a feeling they would be with her for a long time to come.

At the gate, she hesitated again. She had the strangest sensation that someone was watching her, and as she turned, her eyes went immediately to the pool house apartment. Even so early in the morning with sunlight flooding across the courtyard, the covered loggia lay in deep gloom.

Now's your chance, a little voice prodded her. *Go upstairs and knock on that door. Prove to yourself there's nothing to be afraid of.*

She even took a few steps toward the outside staircase, but then froze as that same intuition of danger seized her.

This was crazy, she tried to tell herself. She was standing out in the open in broad daylight. Nothing was going to happen to her if she climbed those stairs, knocked on the door and came face-to-face with the person inside the apartment.

But she couldn't make herself do it. The fear was too strong. Whether she was afraid of the man or the place, she had no idea. But suddenly she couldn't wait to be miles and miles from Cape Diablo.

As she whirled toward the gate, the scream of a hawk overhead made her blood go cold.

SHE EMERGED FROM the mangrove thicket a few minutes later and immediately spotted the supply boat tied up at the end of the pier. A man sat on the wooden planks dangling his feet over the water. When he saw her, he scrambled up and hurried over to meet her.

He was dressed in grungy jeans and an old Lynard Skynard T-shirt that was faded and misshapen from years of wear and tear. Tall and lanky, the new driver was younger than Pete Trawick, and judging by his easy smile, way more pleasant.

"Carrie Bishop?"

She nodded.

"I'm Lee Grady. I understand you need a ride back to the mainland." He held out his hand for her bag.

"Yes, thank you." She glanced around. "Where's Nick? He said he would wait here to make sure you didn't leave without me."

The man glanced around. "I think he mentioned something about needing to get to work."

Carrie wasn't surprised exactly, but she couldn't help feeling a twinge of disappointment that he hadn't even stuck around long enough to say goodbye, especially after the way he'd kissed her last night.

Don't be stupid, she scolded herself. Since when did one kiss mean anything? She might be inexperienced, but she wasn't naive. She just wasn't the type of woman a man like Nick Draco would go for.

Which was for the best because there was still something about him that she couldn't quite bring herself to trust.

Behind that cold, relentless stare lay secrets. Perhaps even dark secrets. The last thing Carrie needed was a man with demons. She had too many of those lurking around in the dark as it was.

After Grady untied the moorings, he hopped down into the boat, stored her bag and then offered her a hand. "Watch your step now."

Carrie climbed aboard and took a seat at the back of the boat. Once they'd cleared the end of the pier, Grady turned the prow into the sun.

Up ahead, as far as Carrie could see lay

nothing but sparkling channels weaving through a vast labyrinth of lush green islands. And at the end of that maze was the mainland and home.

Carrie glanced over her shoulder for one last look at Cape Diablo. The island was beautiful in the morning sun, but she knew that a closer scrutiny would reveal the shadows of the past that grew as dark and thick as the lichen on the crumbling walls of the mansion.

The island had secrets, too, and as the boat moved into the open water, Carrie felt an almost intense sense of relief.

Then she saw Nick up on the roof, and even from a distance, she could feel their gazes connect. Her heart fluttered in awareness as she lifted her hand to wave goodbye. When he didn't respond, she watched for a moment longer, then turned away.

So that was that.

NICK STARED AT THE BOAT until it was nothing but a tiny dot on the horizon before he went back to work. He'd done what he set out to do. He'd gotten Carrie away from Cape Diablo. So why did he feel like crap this morning?

Maybe he should just admit to himself that knowing about her past, what she'd been through, had gotten to him.

And, yeah, maybe the woman herself had gotten to him a little, too.

Her loyalty and determination were qualities he could admire, but they were also apt to get her in trouble if she wasn't careful. Something wasn't right about Tia Falcon's disappearance. Nick had a bad feeling about the whole situation. It was starting to smell a little too much like a setup to him.

He didn't believe in the superstitions surrounding Cape Diablo, but he sure as hell knew better than to ignore his instincts. Maybe it was high time he disregarded his orders and started a little investigation of his own.

THE FIRST THING Carrie did when she got back to the mainland was check her voice mail. She'd left her car in a public lot at the tiny marina in Everglades City, and as she unlocked the trunk to stow her bag, she listened to her messages—two from the magazine and one from the next-door neighbor who'd offered to pick up her mail.

She ignored the ones from work. She wasn't due back into the office until Monday, and she didn't want to get drawn into a problem or some major project that would keep her busy through the weekend.

The message from her neighbor alarmed her, though, and as Carrie climbed into the car, she dialed Mrs. Petersen's number.

"Hi, this is Carrie," she said, when the older woman picked up the phone. "I just got your message."

"Carrie! I was hoping you'd call today. I was getting a little concerned when I didn't hear back from you."

Carrie started the engine and rolled down the windows to allow the trapped heat to escape. "Sorry. I've been out of commission for a couple of days. Is something wrong?"

"I don't think so. But I thought you might want to know that a policeman came by here looking for you yesterday. He wanted to ask you some questions about the break-in."

That didn't make much sense. She'd already told the responding officer everything she knew, which wasn't much. She'd come home from work to find a broken latch on the sliding-glass door in her bedroom. Nothing had been missing that Carrie could determine, but the investigating officer seemed to think the culprit had been scared off by the neighbor's dog.

"Was it Officer Kendal?" Carrie asked.

"No, I met him, too. This was someone different. A Detective Something-or-other. I have his name here somewhere…." Mrs. Petersen's voice trailed off and Carrie could hear her rummaging through papers.

"You say he had more questions about the break-in?" Something about this didn't sound right to Carrie. She didn't like the idea of someone, even a cop, snooping around her apartment while she was away.

"He said there'd been a rash of break-ins in the neighborhood, and he just wanted to follow up on your report, make sure you hadn't had any more problems. He also wanted to check the sliding door where the burglar came in."

"You didn't let him inside my apartment, did you?" Carrie asked sharply.

Her abrupt tone seemed to take Mrs. Petersen aback. When she finally responded, she sounded a little hurt that Carrie would question her judgment. "No, of course I didn't let him. I know better than that. But I'm sure he was on the up-and-up. He was a very pleasant man. Very polite. I know I have his name around here somewhere...."

"Don't worry about it," Carrie said,

trying to make up for her curt tone. "I'm sure it'll turn up. You can give it to me when I get home."

"A MISSING PERSONS REPORT? You'll need to talk to Deputy Malloy," the redheaded receptionist at the Collier County Sheriff's substation in Everglades City told Carrie a little while later. "He's out on a call right now and there's really no telling how long it'll take him. You might want to check back in a couple of hours."

"I don't want to wait that long," Carrie said. "I'm on my way back to Miami, and I want to make sure the report gets filed before I leave here. Isn't there someone else I can talk to?"

"All the other deputies are out on patrol," she said. "We're a little short-handed right now. You'll need to wait for Deputy Malloy or else drive over to the Sheriff's office in Naples and file your report."

Just then a door to one of the back

offices opened and a uniformed deputy stuck his head around the corner. "Annie, how's about a cup of coffee? I'm drowning in paperwork back here. If I don't get some caffeine down me, I'll never make it through all these reports." He saw Carrie then and tipped his head. "Something we can help you with, Miss?"

"She wants to file a missing persons report," the redhead said over her shoulder. "I told her she needs to either talk to Malloy or drive over to Naples to see the sheriff."

"This is ridiculous," Carrie said. "This is a police station, isn't it? There must be someone here I can talk to."

The man gave her a nod. "Come on back. I'm Deputy Polk. Glen Polk," he said shaking her hand. "Missing Persons isn't exactly my specialty, but I can take your statement and pass it along to Malloy when he gets in."

He held the door for Carrie and she walked into a tiny, cramped office littered with stacks of boxes and files. He cleared a chair across from his desk and motioned for her to sit.

"I'm usually involved in aerial surveillance," he explained as he took a seat behind his desk. "Got myself an inner ear problem that's grounded me for a couple of weeks so I'm stuck pushing pencils." He shuffled aside a few papers on his desk before settling in. "Now, why don't you tell me who's missing and I'll see what I can do to help you. Let's start with a name."

"Her name is Tia Falcon and she's a friend of mine," Carrie said. "She came down here about three weeks ago after leasing an apartment on Cape Diablo."

"On Diablo?" A frown flickered across his brow. "Why there?"

"I assume she wanted a quiet place to spend the summer," Carrie said with a shrug.

"We'll need a description," he said, grabbing a pencil to take notes."

"She's twenty-six and about my height…

five feet five. She probably weighs around one fifteen and she has shoulder-length dark hair. I have a picture of her. It's a newspaper clipping so it's not very clear, but it's the only one I have." She dug the clipping out of her purse and passed it to Polk.

He studied it for a moment, then glanced up. "This is an engagement announcement. Is the man with her the husband?"

"Actually, no. They were supposed to get married a few weeks ago, right before Tia came down here. But she called off the ceremony at the last minute."

Polk lifted one brow. "A runaway bride, huh?"

"I guess you could call her that. I haven't heard from her in over two weeks, not since she first came down here. And now she's missing from her apartment. Her clothes are still in the closet and her refrigerator's well stocked, but there's no sign of Tia anywhere. And no one on Cape

Diablo seems to know what happened to her. It's a small island, Deputy. No one saw her leave. No one remembers the last time they saw her. It's all very strange."

"Does she have a history of taking off without telling anyone?"

Carrie hesitated. A couple of times in high school, Tia had run away from home, but that was years ago.

"I take it by your silence that she has. Let me ask you something," he said slowly. "How did she call off the wedding?"

"What do you mean?"

"Was it planned or an impulse? In other words, did she leave the groom standing at the altar?"

"What difference does that make?" Carrie said impatiently.

He sat back in his chair and folded his arms over his chest. "This kind of thing happens more frequently than people realize. A bride gets cold feet and can't go through with the ceremony. But she can't face her family and friends so she takes off. You see where I'm going with this, don't you? If your friend was impulsive enough to leave her groom at the altar, she's probably impulsive enough to take off from Cape Diablo without telling anyone."

"So what you're saying is that you're not going to do anything about this," Carrie said angrily.

"I didn't say that at all. We'll file a report and we'll keep an eye out for her, but if you ask me, you're working yourself up over nothing. My guess is, she and her fiancé had a fight the night before the wedding and she took off to teach him a lesson. When she thinks he's suffered long enough, she'll turn up. They may even go ahead with the ceremony."

"You don't know how much I wish that were true," Carrie said. "But, unfortunately, I think you're dead wrong, Deputy."

ERMA PETERSEN WAS a New Jersey snowbird who'd come south for the winter twenty years ago and never left. She was a tiny, white-haired dynamo who kept fit and tanned by playing eighteen holes of golf every day, rain or shine, but knee surgery had left her housebound for the past two months and she'd become something of a busybody in the apartment complex.

However, she meant well, and since Carrie didn't really know any of her other neighbors well enough to ask for favors, she was glad to have someone nearby who didn't seem to mind picking up her mail and keeping an eye on her place while she was away.

"I found it," Mrs. Petersen said in triumph when she opened the door to Carrie a little while later. She waved a piece of paper through the air. "I found the name of that policeman right after you hung up. It was there on the table where I put it, but I'd forget my head if it wasn't attached. His name is Davis." She handed the note to Carrie. "Detective Raymond Davis. See?"

Carrie glanced at the scribbled name.

"He didn't give you a card?" she asked suspiciously.

"He said he left them in another jacket."

"Did you ask to see his identification?"

Mrs. Petersen gave her an affronted look. "Well, of course, dear. I'm not completely stupid, contrary to what some people around here seem to think."

"I'm sorry. I didn't mean to imply that you were," Carrie said contritely. "I'm just a little anxious about the break-in." She paused, trying once again to soothe the older woman's ruffled feathers. "What did he look like?"

"Tall, thin, clean-cut." Mrs. Petersen gave her a knowing look. "Quite attractive really. And very charming. I'd even say charismatic."

Carrie thought instantly of Trey Hollinger. She fished out the engagement picture she'd shown Deputy Polk. He'd made a copy before she left the office and given her back the original. "Is this the man?" she asked anxiously.

Mrs. Petersen took the picture and gave it a quick perusal. "No, I don't think so." She took a second look, then glanced up at Carrie. "You certainly seem suspicious, Carrie. Is there something you're not telling me?"

"I just find it odd that he didn't have a card. And I don't know what more the police could want from me because I've already told them everything I know."

"I didn't let him into your apartment if you're still worrying about that," Mrs. Petersen said primly.

"I know. And I'm sorry that I snapped at you on the phone. Like I said, all this business has me a little nervous."

Mrs. Petersen accepted the explanation and nodded as she reached for the stack of mail on the hallway table. "That's understandable. I've been a little on edge myself lately. Milo's dog has been barking at all hours, and I keep imaging that someone's outside snooping around. I haven't been able to sleep a wink. It gives me the chills thinking about some creep skulking about the complex while we lie sleeping in our beds." She shuddered. "Lots of crazies out there these days. A woman can't be too careful."

You have no idea, Carrie thought as she took her mail and said goodbye.

Letting herself into her apartment, she closed and locked the door, then stood looking around for a moment. She'd only been gone since Tuesday, but already her apartment had that funny, abandoned smell that came when all the doors and windows had been shut up too long.

Crossing over to her desk, she dumped the mail in a drawer, then picked up the phone and called the police department.

"I'd like to speak to Detective Raymond Davis," she said, when her call was finally answered.

She half expected to be told that there was no one at the station by that name, but after a few seconds, the line clicked and a masculine voice said gruffly, "This is Davis."

"Detective Raymond Davis?" Carrie asked in surprise.

"One and the same."

"My name is Carrie Bishop. I live in the Brook Hollow apartments on Sea Crest Boulevard. My next-door neighbor said you came by looking for me yesterday."

"Hold on."

She heard him rifle through papers, then he said, "Right. You reported a break-in at your apartment on the six-teenth of this month."

"Yes, I did. Do you have news about the case?" Carrie asked anxiously.

"No, but like I told your neighbor, there's been a number of similar incidents in that area recently. I was hoping you might remember something that you'd left out of your original statement. Sometimes it happens that way."

"I'm sorry," Carrie said. "But I wasn't even home at the time of the break-in. I didn't see anything."

"I understand, but we'd really like to

catch this guy," Davis said wearily. "If you do remember something or you see any suspicious characters around in the neighborhood, you give us a call immediately."

"I will. And thanks for the follow-up, Detective."

"That's what I'm here for."

Carrie hung up, relieved to know that Raymond Davis really was a cop, even though there'd been no progress in her case.

Sitting down at the desk, Carrie opened her laptop, plugged in her digital camera, and uploaded the shots from Cape Diablo. Most of them had been taken when she and Nick searched the island, but a few of them were of the courtyard and pool.

She couldn't help remembering both Alma and Carlos gazing into those murky depths as if they could see something beneath the surface that no one else could.

Carrie skimmed through all the images until she came to the one she'd taken of the upstairs apartment and loggia. Peering at the image, she saw something that she hadn't seen the first time she browsed through them. Someone stood in the shadows. She could see nothing more than a silhouette, certainly no features, but the camera had caught something....

Was it Ethan Stone?

Carrie enlarged the image and used a photo enhancement tool to try to sharpen the contrast, but the shadows were too deep. She couldn't make out the face.

Printing off all the shots on photographic paper, she stacked them up on her desk, then got up and carried her bag into the bathroom.

Peeling off her clothes, she threw everything into the hamper, then climbed into the shower and stood under the spray for a very long time.

She still couldn't help wondering why Nick hadn't waited to tell her goodbye that morning. She'd probably never see him again, and the sooner she put him out of her head the better, but he might have at least waited to see her off.

Carrie didn't understand why she couldn't stop thinking about him. It was as if she'd never been infatuated with a man before. She was no stranger to sexual attraction, but she'd always kept a wall between her emotions and her desires. It was one thing to be physically drawn to someone, quite another to fall in love with him.

Not that she was in love with Nick Draco. She didn't even know him, and even more, she didn't quite trust him. Still, she had a feeling it was going to be a very long time before she forgot the way he'd looked at her last night just before he kissed her.

He'd wanted her, and he'd made her want him in a way that had caught her completely off guard. She enjoyed sex, but she didn't like losing control, and Nick Draco was the kind of man that could turn a woman inside out. Carrie wasn't at all certain she could handle that kind of intensity.

Stepping out of the shower, she toweled off, then took her time drying her hair and putting away the toiletries she'd taken with her to Cape Diablo. Pulling on clean jeans and an apple-green tank top, she went out to the kitchen to see what she could find to eat.

The afternoon sunlight streamed in through the window above her desk and light flashed on something metal. Carrie thought at first it was merely a pen or a paper clip she'd left lying about, but as she walked past the desk to the kitchen, she stopped short, backtracked, and then caught her breath in recognition.

The breakaway heart pendant lying on top of the photo of the loggia was a perfect match to the one she'd found on the floor in Tia's bedroom. But it wasn't the same pendant. This one was inscribed with the word *Friends* and the edges of the metal had been worn down.

This pendant had been taken from the jewelry box in her bedroom and brought out here only a few short minutes ago while she'd been in the shower.

Chapter Eleven

Her heart pounding in terror, Carrie spun and frantically searched the corners for a shadow or a movement. He could still be inside, she thought desperately. He could be hiding in her closet or underneath her bed....

She didn't wait to find out.

Grabbing the necklace and the photos, she scooped up her bag and rushed out the door. Hurrying across the hallway, she banged on Mrs. Petersen's door, but when she didn't immediately answer, Carrie gave up.

She didn't waste time trying any of the other doors. Most everyone would still be at work. Mrs. Petersen was the only one in the building who was home all day, and she'd obviously stepped out. Carrie could scream and scream and no one would come running.

Her first instinct was to get out of the building. Someone was bound to be about outside. The groundskeeper, a jogger, *someone*.

She shot out the front door and didn't stop until she reached her car in the covered parking lot. Using the remote, she quickly climbed inside and then pressed the lock button.

Out of breath, her heart still racing, she stared out the windows, trying to spot someone who might have followed her out of the building.

She didn't see anyone.

But no way had she imagined this. No way had she simply overlooked the pendant earlier. The heart had been stored in the bottom of her jewelry box for years. Someone had been in her apartment. Someone who knew what he was looking for because he'd probably been in there before.

Carrie felt weak with fear. The idea of that monster being in her apartment, going through her things…

If he'd been that close, why had he left her alone? She'd been vulnerable in the shower. He could have snuck into the bathroom and she never would have heard him. He could have done anything and no one would have heard a thing.

So why hadn't he?

Because he wasn't ready. He was toying with her, playing some sort of sick game. He was leading her on a wild-goose chase looking for Tia when all along she might already be dead.

But Carrie wouldn't allow herself to believe that. Tia was alive and she was still on Cape Diablo.

And Carrie knew what she had to do to save her.

"I NEED TO HIRE a boat to take me to Cape Diablo as soon as possible."

The man Carrie had approached at the marina in Everglades City was busy untangling a fishing line. He didn't even look up when he answered her. "Be cheaper if you wait until morning and catch the supply boat."

"I can't wait until morning." She tried to keep her urgency under control, but Carrie's instincts were telling her that time was running out for Tia. She had to get to Cape Diablo tonight! "Besides, the supply boat already ran today."

He kept right on working at a knot. "Nope, supply boat runs out to Diablo on Tuesdays and Fridays. Today's Thursday."

"I know what day it is," Carrie said impatiently. "Pete Trawick had some sort of engine trouble so his cousin took over for him. He made the run today instead of tomorrow. So I couldn't catch the supply boat even if I wanted to."

The man looked up then and squinted in

the late-afternoon sunlight. He was around sixty or so with skin the color and texture of aged leather. "I saw Trawick not more than a couple of hours ago. Talked to him myself. He didn't say anything about boat trouble. And as far as I know, he's got no kin."

Carrie frowned. "I'm telling you someone brought supplies out to the island this morning because I was there. I saw him. I even rode back to the marina with him. He said his name was Lee Grady, and I understood that he was somehow related to Mr. Trawick."

The man shook his head. "I've known Pete all his life, and I'm telling *you,* he doesn't have any family. Least not in these parts. And I've never even heard of this Lee Grady fellow, and I pretty much know everyone around here. So looks like someone's been pulling your leg, little lady."

That or someone had gone to a great deal of trouble to get her off the island, Carrie thought grimly. She was being pulled in two different directions. Apparently someone wanted her off the island while the demons of her past kept luring her back. "Do you know of a driver that would be willing to take me out to Cape Diablo tonight?"

He gave her a doubtful look. "Might not be that easy. Come dark, people get mighty superstitious of that place."

"I'll double the usual fee," Carrie said. "Whatever it takes."

The man nodded. "Well, now you're talking the right language. Greenbacks do have a way of boosting courage." He finally gave up on the fishing line and tossed it aside. "Tell you what. My nephew has a boat. He's usually looking to make a few extra bucks, but he works for the county. He won't get off until after five, then it'll take him a while to drive over here. If you're willing to wait that long, I can give him a call."

Carrie nodded. "That's fine. Just please tell him to get here as quickly as he can."

"If you want to grab a bite to eat while I call him, you can wait inside the café. Can't say the food is all that great, but it'll get you out of the heat."

"Thanks."

Carrie walked across the street and entered the tiny restaurant. The place was almost empty so she had her choice of seats. She took a booth by the window where she could watch the marina.

After a moment or two, a blond waitress in jeans and a Florida State T-shirt came to take her order. "Just coffee," Carrie told her.

"Be right back."

When the waitress brought back the carafe, Carrie said, "You have a great view of the marina here. I'll bet you enjoy seeing all the boats come and go."

The woman couldn't have looked more bored. "I guess so. I don't pay much attention to them anymore."

"You've worked here for a while then," Carrie said.

The woman grimaced. "Too damn long."

"Do you get many tourists in here?"

"Depends on the time of year." The woman scratched her head with her pencil. "Sure you don't want something to eat?"

"No, coffee's fine."

The woman hesitated, then said curiously, "So what brings you down here? Sightseeing?"

"Actually, no. I'm here looking for a friend of mine. I haven't heard from her in a couple of weeks and I'm starting to get a little worried. I wonder if you might have seen her around." Carrie pulled out the engagement photograph and laid it on the table.

"That's her?" The waitress picked up the picture and studied it for a moment, her brow knitting in concentration.

"Do you recognize her?"

"Not her, no." She placed the picture back on the table and put her index finger over Trey Hollinger's face. "I've seen him, though. He came in a few days ago looking for a driver to take him to Cape Diablo."

"Are you sure?" Carrie asked in shock. "You're positive it was him?"

"Yeah, I'm real good with faces, and besides, this guy was pretty unforgettable if you know what I mean. Good-looking, charming, big tipper."

"Did he say anything else? Did he tell you why he was here?"

"Mentioned something about fishing. Didn't look the type if you ask me, but…" She shrugged. "He left a twenty-dollar bill for a two-dollar cup of coffee so what do I care why he's here."

So TREY HOLLINGER had come to Cape Diablo looking for Tia. Somehow he'd found out where she was and he'd followed her.

Carrie stared out over the bow at the waves, deep gold in the fading sunlight, and thought back to her first trip to the island. Cochburn had told her that the only other tenant was a burned-out executive named Ethan Stone who'd rented the upstairs apartment a few days before Carrie had arrived. Cochburn had never met the man because a secretary had made all the arrangements.

It was the perfect setup if Trey had wanted to keep a low profile. If he hadn't wanted anyone to be able to trace his whereabouts to Cape Diablo.

Maybe her first instinct about Trey Hollinger had been right. He wasn't a man to take rejection lightly. Carrie could well imagine him following Tia to the island and confronting her. If his temper had exploded the way it had at the church that day...

Carrie shuddered. He was a violent man, but also a very clever one. He knew how to cover his tracks.

By the time the boat finally arrived at Cape Diablo, twilight had fallen. There were no lights on in the apartment over Tia's, and Carrie stood in the courtyard for a moment, trying to decide how best to confront Trey…if in fact he and Ethan Stone were one and the same person.

Should she wait until morning…or do it now and catch him off guard.

Drawing a deep breath, she started for the stairs. She put her hand on the banister and froze as she sensed someone had come up behind her. Whirling, she gasped when she saw a tall shadow emerge from the rest.

Then her hand flew to her heart. "Nick!"

He walked toward her slowly. "What are you doing back here?"

She glanced up at the apartment, then lowered her voice. "I told you this morning I couldn't leave without knowing Tia was okay. I had to come back and find her."

She took his arm and pulled him back into the shadows.

"I was right about Trey Hollinger," she said excitedly. "A waitress in Everglades City saw him a few days ago. He was looking for a boat to bring him here to the island. I think he used an alias to rent the apartment above Tia's. He knows where she is."

Nick glared at her. "And what are you planning to do? March up there and confront him?"

"Yes!"

"That's not a good idea."

"Why not?"

He paused. "You shouldn't have come back here, Carrie."

Something in his voice sent a chill up her spine. "Why not?" When he didn't answer, she said in shock, "It was you, wasn't it? You're the one who wanted me off the island. You made up that whole story about Trawick having boat trouble. *Why?*"

"You ask too many questions," he said grimly. "You should have left well enough alone."

Suddenly everything became crystal clear to Carrie. "Last night when I saw you down by the harbor. That wasn't just an accident, was it? You were on your way to meet those men."

Even in the moonlight, she could see his features harden, and a thrill of fear chased down her spine. "If you believe that, you're either incredibly naive or incredibly stupid to have come back here."

"If you're not mixed up with those men, then why did you want me off the island?"

"Because it's not safe here." He flicked another glance toward the stairs. "Come back with me to my place. We need to have a talk."

Carrie hesitated. Something told her she wasn't going to want to hear what he had to say, but she followed him out of the courtyard anyway.

"I WORK FOR THE Joint Intelligence Task Force in Key West." They were standing in Nick's tiny living room because Carrie had refused to sit.

"Just get it over with," she'd blurted. *"Tell me what it is you have to say."*

Now she stared at him in shock. "You're a *cop?*" She hadn't expected that.

"I'm a federal agent. I was sent here to investigate a recent Intel report about a sudden rise in drug trafficking in the Mangrove Islands. And Cape Diablo seems to be at the center of it."

"I don't understand," Carrie said in confusion. "If you're an agent, why didn't you arrest those men last night? You caught them red-handed."

He gave her a wry smile. "I was pretty badly outnumbered in case you didn't notice. And besides, we're not after the locals. We want the guys who are financing this operation. That's why it's imperative that I maintain a low profile. If they get wind that we're onto them, they'll just move the operation someplace else."

Carrie drew a breath. "So that's why you didn't want me going to the police."

He nodded. "If the cops start sniffing

around the island, these guys will just disappear and we'll lose our window of opportunity."

"And you wanted me off the island because—"

"Like I said, you ask too many questions."

Carrie absorbed that for a minute. Then she looked at him aghast. "What about Tia? Is that why you tried so hard to convince me that she'd gone back to the mainland? Because you didn't want me asking questions?"

"We don't know that she hasn't gone back—"

"Stop. Just stop!" Carrie said angrily. "You believed what you wanted to believe because it was more convenient for you. You didn't care about her safety. You didn't care if I found her or not. You just didn't want me bringing the cops here to search the island."

When he didn't deny it, Carrie spun toward the door, but he caught her arm.

"You can't do this on your own. It's too dangerous. Let me help you."

"It's too late for that. I don't trust you, Nick, and I don't want your help," she said bitterly. "I'll find Tia on my own. You just stay out of my way."

BUT HE FOLLOWED HER back to the apartment anyway, and when Carrie started up the steps, he caught her arm. "Wait here. Let me go up first."

For the first time, Carrie saw that he had his gun drawn. She wanted to send him away, but the sight of that weapon was more comforting than she wanted to admit.

So was Nick's presence. She didn't trust him, and she was mad as hell at him for putting his own interests ahead of Tia's, but she also knew that he was right. She had no business confronting Trey Hollinger alone and unarmed. She'd seen first-hand how quickly his temper could erupt.

She wouldn't wait behind, though. She

followed Nick up the stairs and glanced around the loggia. The shadows underneath the cover had deepened to black.

Peering into the darkness, she could see nothing at all in the corners. No stealthy movement. No red eyes glowing from the gloom.

She waited for the premonition of danger to overwhelm her again, but tonight something was different. Maybe it was because she knew who was inside the apartment now and could put a face on her irrational fear. But more likely, it was because of Nick.

Turning her back on the shadows, she watched as Nick pounded on the door.

To her amazement, the door swung inward.

Nick glanced over his shoulder and motioned for her to stay put. When Carrie shook her head, he rolled his eyes and stepped across the threshold.

"Stone? You in here? Nick Draco. I'm a federal agent. I'd like to ask you some questions."

Nothing but silence.

Nick found the light switch and flipped it. Carrie blinked at the sudden brilliance, then gazed around. The layout and furnishings were almost identical to the space downstairs. It was neat and clean with the barest trace of bleach clinging to the air.

Where was Trey? He had to be here somewhere. As they moved down the hall to the bedroom, Carrie could already smell the cloying scent of his cologne.

Nick walked into the bedroom and turned on the light. "Doesn't look like he's here."

But he hadn't gone far, Carrie thought. His keys, watch and pinkie ring lay on the dresser. Something sparkled amidst the cache of metal, and as she walked over to take a closer look, she caught her breath. It was Tia's engagement ring.

"That's Tia's ring," she whispered. "She had it on at the church, so that means—"

A sound came from somewhere nearby, and Trey put a finger to his lips. Weapon still drawn, he slipped out of the room and a moment later, Carrie heard his footsteps pounding down the stairs.

He must have spotted Trey, Carrie thought as she started to go after him. Then her attention was caught by something on the floor underneath the edge of the bed.

A woman's white shoe. And it was covered in blood.

Dear God, it was Tia's shoe.

Her chest tightening in trepidation, she knelt and peered under the bed. Nothing…

But Tia had been in here. Carrie was certain of it now.

She went over and pulled open the closet door. Trey's clothes were lined up neatly on the rod, but what drew Carrie's attention—what made her gasp out loud— was the huge roll of plastic lying on the floor.

And through the clear layers, Carrie saw something that might have been a face….

Chapter Twelve

She screamed and as she tried to scramble away, she fell against the bed and slipped to the floor.

Oh, God, Oh, God, Oh, God, she silent prayed as she struggled to her feet and rushed through the apartment. She'd left the front door open and now she saw someone standing on the threshold blocking her way.

Carrie screamed again a split second before she recognized Nick.

Then she launched herself toward him and he caught her by her arms. "Are you all right? Sorry I left you alone like that, but I saw someone in the courtyard. It was only Alma—" His voice broke off when he saw her face. "My God, Carrie, what is it?"

She was trembling so hard she could barely speak. "A body…in the closet. Oh, God, I think…I think it's Tia."

NICK USED HIS SATELLITE phone to summon the police. It took less than an hour for a marine patrol boat to arrive from the Collier County Sheriff's office, but another two hours before a forensics team and a criminal investigator were on the scene.

In the meantime, Nick had led Carrie downstairs to Tia's apartment and sat with her while she gave her statement to the responding officer. He hadn't left her side for a moment, and now as Carrie watched the body, still wrapped in plastic, being carried downstairs, she felt his arm slip around her shoulders.

"You okay?"

She shook her head. "I don't think I am."

"Just hang in there a little longer," he said.

They placed the body in the courtyard by the pool, and one of the deputies came over to knock on the door. Nick left Carrie long enough to let him in. "We need to see if one of you can identify the body," he said.

"I'll do it," Nick said quickly.

"No, I need to do this," Carrie said.

"You sure?"

She nodded and stood. She was still a little unsteady, and Nick took her arm. In the time between her finding the body and when the police arrived on the scene, she and Nick had called an unspoken truce. His earlier deception didn't seem to matter much now in light of her grisly discovery.

Tia was dead.

She was dead because Trey Hollinger had followed her to Cape Diablo and killed her.

Carrie still couldn't believe it, and yet a part of her had always known what the man was capable of.

Outside, one of the deputies had already

split open the plastic. Even in the open
night air, the smell was overwhelming,
and Carrie had to hold back her retching
reflex as she slowly walked toward the
body.

As she neared, the deputy who had been
kneeling over the plastic stood and moved
out of her way. Carrie braced herself and
glanced down.

It wasn't Tia.

It wasn't Tia.

Her legs went weak with relief and she
couldn't seem to comprehend anything
else for a moment.

It wasn't Tia.

It was Trey Hollinger.

She hadn't recognized him at first. His
handsome face had been badly disfig-
ured by decomposition and by the
killer's knife.

"Oh, my God." She put a hand to her
mouth, choking back a wave of nausea.

"Do you know this man?" one of the
deputies questioned her.

She nodded weakly. "His name is Trey Hollinger. He's from Miami."

"Do you have any idea what he was doing on Cape Diablo?"

"He must have come here looking for Tia."

"The missing friend? The one you thought was in the plastic?"

Carrie nodded again.

"You said she came here because she was running away from this guy," the deputy said slowly.

"That's what I thought." Carrie was shaking so hard she could hardly speak.

"And now he's dead and she's missing."

Something in his tone made Carrie glance at him in outrage. "You can't think she did this?"

The deputy's eyes were on the body. "Whoever killed this guy had one helluva a grudge. The body's practically cut to ribbons."

Carrie's stomach lurched. "It wasn't Tia. She could never do something like that."

"Not even if she was threatened?"

"No!" Carrie put a trembling hand to her mouth. "I should have said something earlier, but I wasn't thinking—"

The deputy gave her a puzzled frown. "What are you talking about?"

"I know who did this."

The deputy's voice sharpened. "You know the identity of the killer?"

Carrie drew a shaky breath. "I don't know his name. Fourteen years ago he called himself Nathaniel Glover." As quickly as she could, she told them the rest of the story.

When she finished, Nick had moved up behind her. He wasn't touching her, but she could feel his presence just the same.

Don't worry, he seemed to be telling her. *I've got your back. Nothing's going to happen to you while I'm around.*

But it was only a false sense of security, and Carrie didn't want to trust it. She was better off *not* trusting it.

"He's come back for us both," Carrie

said in a whisper. "He already has Tia. And now he's using her to get to me." Whether they believed her or not, Carrie had no idea. But she knew. Somewhere on this island, he watched and he waited.

"I always like saving the best for last."

"We'll leave a boat to patrol the perimeter overnight," the deputy was saying. "No one's leaving the island without us knowing about it. First thing in the morning, we'll bring a K-9 unit and search every square inch of this place."

"What about Tia?" Carrie asked fearfully.

"Don't worry. If she's still on the island the dogs will find her." He paused. "Shouldn't take that long, either."

BACK INSIDE THE APARTMENT, Carrie paced in front of the windows and Nick watched her from his place on the couch. She was still badly shaken and would be for hours.

And she was still in denial, too. The deputy had made a good point, one that Nick had thought of almost instantly. Trey

Hollinger was dead and Tia was missing. Her belongings were still in the apartment, leading any good investigator to conclude that she'd left the island in a hurry.

He said none of this to Carrie, however, because she wasn't ready to accept the possibility that her friend could be a killer. Carrie's judgment would probably always be clouded where Tia was concerned because of the past and what they'd been through together. But sooner or later she would have to face the fact that the Tia she knew might never be coming back.

"Why don't you go to bed and try to get some sleep," he said. "Tomorrow will be a long day and you already look exhausted." If the police found Tia's body, Carrie would need all her strength to get through the ordeal, and if they found her alive—

"I don't want to go to sleep," Carrie said. "I don't want the nightmares to come back."

He got up and went over to the window

where she stood. "Do you want to talk about it?"

She shook her head. "You heard everything outside. There's nothing more to tell."

He had a feeling that was far from the truth. "The offer stands. How about something to eat?"

"I'm not hungry." Carrie folded her arms across her middle as if she were suddenly chilled. Her eyes looked lost and haunted. "I left her there, Nick. I ran away and left her with that monster. When I think about what he did to her…what he might be doing to her even now…" She put her hands to her face and squeezed her eyes closed.

Nick took her hands and gently pried them away. "You were just a kid. You did what you had to do. If you hadn't gotten away, he would have killed you both."

"I know that. Logically, I know that, but what happened that day was all my fault. I've never been able to forgive myself for what I caused. And now if I can't find her in time…" She broke off. "I have to find her, Nick. I have to."

"We will." One way or another, he thought grimly.

She turned back to the window. "Tell me about your job, your past, anything. I don't care. Just talk."

"I have a brother who's in prison," he said. "How's that for starters?"

She turned in surprise. "What's he in for?"

"Cocaine trafficking and possession with the intent to sell."

Carrie's eyes widened. "But you—"

"Yeah. We don't really get along," he said dryly. "In fact, I haven't seen him in years. I used to drive out to the prison once a week, but he never would see me so I stopped going."

"Why wouldn't he see you?"

Nick's voice hardened. "Because I'm the one who busted him."

He could tell she was taken aback by that little revelation. "What happened?"

"I used to be a cop in Miami," he said.

"I was an undercover narc. I was working a sting operation on some local dealers. We'd engineered a big buy and my brother arrived with the sellers. I didn't even know he was still in Miami. We'd lost touch years earlier, and last I'd heard he was working down in the Keys. Anyway, he showed up, recognized me and blew my cover. So much for blood being thicker than water," he muttered.

"So you sent him to prison," Carrie said.

"I made the arrest and testified against him at his trial. He's the one who put himself in prison."

"Of course. I didn't mean to imply…" She trailed off.

Nick shrugged. "It's okay. I used to blame myself for what happened to him. Told myself I should have looked after him better because I was older, more experienced. Our parents were killed in a wreck when we were kids and we went to live with our grandmother. She was too old to have to deal with two teenage boys, and she pretty much let us run wild. Matt got in with a bad crowd. He dropped out of high school, started using drugs. I caught him stealing money out of our grandmother's purse when he was sixteen years old. She'd just cashed her social security check that day, and he didn't even care that the money was all she had to live on for a month. All he cared about was his next fix.

"Instead of trying to help him, I kicked him out of the house and washed my hands of him. He was arrested a week later on his first drug charge. After that, it was just one thing after another."

"You shouldn't blame yourself," Carrie said. "It wasn't your fault."

"I know that now. Just like what happened to Tia wasn't your fault." He came over and put his hands on her shoulder. "You have to let the guilt go. It'll eat you up inside if you don't."

"But how do I do that," she whispered desperately. "How do I let it go? It's all I know."

"You have to tear down some of the walls," he said. "Let something else in besides guilt."

"Is that what you did?"

"Took a while but yeah, I finally figured it out."

Carrie moved away from him for a moment. "Have you ever been married, Nick?"

He shrugged. "No."

"Engaged?

"No, why?"

"Maybe you haven't torn down as many of the walls as you think."

"Or maybe I just haven't found the right woman."

His eyes seemed to deepen as he watched her, and Carrie caught her breath. "Nick?"

"Yeah."

"Do you want to make love to me?"

One brow lifted in surprise. "Oh, yeah. But I'm not sure that's such a good idea."

"Why not?"

"Maybe tonight's not the best time to

start tearing down the walls," he said. "You've been through a lot today. Your emotions are still ragged. You shouldn't act on impulses."

"But I want to act on impulse," she said softly. "And I want to feel something tonight besides guilt."

She cupped the back of his neck and pulled him toward her. She was afraid at first that he might resist, but when his lips touched hers, something seemed to explode inside both of them. Nick groaned, drawing her to him, and Carrie wrapped her arms around his neck as he lifted her and carried her into the bedroom. They undressed each other between kisses.

When they were naked, Carrie lay back against the pillows and Nick stood at the foot of the bed, gazing down at her. Then kneeling, he slid his hands up the insides of her legs, stroking her gently until Carrie began to tremble all over.

She wasn't so sure about this now. She'd

never liked losing control, and now she found herself perilously close to the edge.

He moved over her, his body touching hers so erotically that Carrie could hardly breathe. "Nick—"

"Shush." He feathered his lips across hers. "Don't talk. Just feel."

His mouth moved down her throat, pressing against her pulse and then finding her breasts. Desire shot through Carrie and she arched her back, moaning softly.

He slid downward, his lips skimming lower and lower until he was kissing her where his fingers had stroked earlier and Carrie responded in a way she'd never believed possible.

She moaned again, a low, erotic sound that both thrilled and scared her. She couldn't seem to stop shaking. She'd never let anyone do this to her before. Intercourse could be a sterile undertaking if one chose it to be, but this…was too intimate. It made her too vulnerable. She wanted to push him away, but she couldn't because already the pressure was building and building.

When her climax erupted, Carrie was rocked all the way to her core. She grabbed Nick's shoulders and pulled him up to her so that she could hang on to him for dear life as the shudders continued to shatter her.

He slid inside her, and when she became tense, he smoothed back her hair and murmured against her lips, "Relax, okay? We're just getting started...."

He moved slowly at first so that Carrie had time to adjust to his body. And then as she began to respond, as her groans became more frenzied, his thrusts deepened.

They exploded together this time, and Nick collapsed on top of her, his breathing as ragged as hers. She could feel his heart beating against hers, and she wondered if it had been as good for him as it had for her. For some reason, she didn't dare ask him. She didn't want anything to ruin the moment.

After a bit, he slid off her and pulled her against him. He pushed back her hair and kissed her neck. "You okay?"

She sighed. "I'm good."

And she was. For the first time in a long time, she wasn't even afraid of the dark.

SOMETIME LATER they got up and showered and then climbed back into bed. Carrie had never spent the night with a man before. If a boyfriend was at her place, she always sent him home. If she was at his, she always got up and slipped quietly away while he slept.

She wasn't about to send Nick away, and he seemed in no hurry to go. He climbed under the covers and pulled her to him again. "You smell good," he murmured. He sounded half-asleep.

Carrie was relieved she wasn't expected to make small talk. She just wanted to lie in his arms and savor the quiet. After a bit, she drifted off, and when she woke up, she caught Nick slipping out of bed.

Disappointment darted through her, but when he saw that she was awake, he put his finger to his lips. Bending over the bed, he said in her ear, "I heard something outside. Stay put while I check it out."

Carrie's heart started to pound in alarm as she watched him glide through the darkness. He'd already pulled on his jeans, and now in the moonlight, she saw that he had his gun drawn. He opened the French door and slipped like a shadow into the overgrown garden.

Pulling on her robe, Carrie padded over to the door. She drew it open slightly, peering out into the darkness. There was moonlight in the garden, but the shadows were so deep she couldn't make anything out. As she stood listening to the dark, she heard a groan, followed by the thud of a body hitting the ground.

"Nick?" She whispered his name frantically, but he didn't respond. "Nick?"

She started to go after him, but a soft whisper of a sound made her heart stop.

Someone was in the room with her. She could feel him behind her, but before she could turn, he grabbed her and pulled her against him.

Shoving a rag against her nose and mouth, he said in a raspy voice, "Told you I'd come back. I always did like saving the best for last."

Chapter Thirteen

When Carrie came to, someone was peering down at her in the darkness. "Nick?"

"No, it's me. Tia."

"Tia?" Carrie thought she was dreaming at first, but when she blinked, the image didn't go away. "It is you! You're alive…."

She tried to sit up again, but her head spun from the ether and she fell back against the hard floor.

She whispered Tia's name again.

"I'm here, Carrie."

"Oh, God, I was so afraid…."

"I knew you'd come," Tia whispered. "I knew you wouldn't leave me here."

Fighting off the nausea, Carrie sat up and looked around. "Where are we?"

"I think we're in the cellar," Tia said. "He drugged me, too. When I woke up, he'd locked me in here." Her voice trailed off a tremor of fear.

Carrie grabbed her hand. "It's him, isn't it?"

Tia nodded. Carrie could see her tear-streaked face in a sliver of moonlight that streamed in from a high window. She glanced around again. "How long have you been in here?"

"I don't know. Days…"

That day she'd followed Alma into the cellar—she must have come so close to finding Tia, Carrie thought. "How did he know where to find you?"

Tia closed her eyes. "He's had someone keeping track of us for years. When he got out of prison, he came to find us. I saw him on the street one day, but I thought the stress of the wedding was making me imagine things. And then I saw him again on my way to the church. He was standing on the street and when he saw me, he started laughing. I was terrified of what he would do to Trey. So I ran away."

"He followed you here?"

"Not at first. He came later."

The break-in, Carrie thought. He'd gotten inside her apartment and found the letter Tia had written. That's how he'd traced her.

"He knew you'd come, too, Carrie. That's why he's kept me alive."

Carrie put her hands on her friend's shoulder. "We'll find a way out of here. I won't let him hurt you again."

Tia nodded. "I know. And I think there is a way out. I found it just before he brought you here."

She scrambled across the room to what looked like a vent. Carrie followed more slowly, still under the influence of the drug. "What is it?"

"I've done a lot of research on this island," Tia said excitedly. "I don't know why I didn't see it before. I've been over this room a hundred times since he put me in here…." She placed her fingers through the wires of the metal grid and tugged. The covering came off, and Carrie peered into a yawning black hole.

"It's a tunnel," Tia said in triumph. "Andres Santiago had it dug when he built the place so that he could slip in and out of the house without being seen. The police found it when they came out here to investigate the family's disappearance."

"Do you know where it comes out?" Carrie asked, her tone anxious.

"No, but does it matter? It's our only way out."

Carrie wished that her head would clear. She wasn't certain this was such a good idea. The tunnel could be blocked on the other end. Or it could be a trap. It seemed too easy somehow.

"Tia, I'm not sure about this. Something doesn't seem right. He could be leading us into a trap."

"I know. I thought about that, too. It does seem too easy. But what choice do we have?"

She crawled into the tunnel and Carrie followed her. It was narrow and pitch-black. Carrie had never suffered from claustrophobia but she had a terrible vision of those walls caving in on them. No one would ever find their bodies. Even Nick wouldn't know where to look....

Nick!

Oh, God, Nick. Where was he? Was he all right? Or was he lying hurt somewhere, maybe even dead....

Carrie wouldn't think about that now. She *couldn't* think about that now.

Tia was still alive, and Carrie had to make sure she stayed that way. This time, they would both get away.

They finally emerged from the tunnel and Tia reached down to offer Carrie a hand. When they were both out in the open, Carrie gazed around, looking for a familiar landmark.

Tia grabbed her hand. "This way!"

Carrie had no idea where they were or where they were headed as she rushed headlong through the mangrove forest behind Tia. And then suddenly she knew exactly where they were and she came to an abrupt halt.

"Tia, wait!"

Her friend slowed and glanced over her shoulder. "Come on! We don't have much time...."

"You're going toward the swamp," Carrie said. *Veer right and it'll take you to the harbor.* It was almost as if Nick were behind her, telling her which way to go.

"Tia, this way!"

But her friend had stopped and was looking in horror over Carrie's shoulder. "He's coming!"

And then Carrie heard it, too. Someone crashing through the trees behind them. Tia grabbed her hand. "Hurry!"

Mud and vines sucked at Carrie's feet as they plunged deeper into the swamp. After a while, she was lost. When Tia stopped to catch her breath, Carrie said, "There's a boat patrolling around the island. We have to make it down to the water and somehow flag him down."

"A boat patrolling the water?" Tia asked in surprise. "Why?" When Carrie hesitated, Tia said softly, "It's Trey, isn't it? They found his body."

"You know about him?" Carrie said in shock.

"Yeah, I know. But he shouldn't have followed me down here, Carrie. He was going to ruin everything. I had to get rid of him."

Carrie gasped. "What are you talking about?"

"I killed Trey," she said, her tone calm. "I was never going to marry him anyway, you know. The wedding was merely an excuse to bring you back into my life."

Carrie's heart was pounding so hard now she could barely breathe. *"Why?"*

"You know why. You left me there. Do

you know what he did to me, Carrie? You can't possibly know. You can't even imagine…." She stopped and drew a breath. "And now it's my turn. Now I'm leaving you behind."

Carrie tried to take a step back from her, but she couldn't move and now she could feel the mud sucking at her feet. And then Nick's warning came back to her.

"*…you may not know you're in it until you feel the mud sucking at your feet. By then it's too late. You're already stuck and the harder you struggle, the quicker you sink.*"

She glanced up and only then did Carrie realize that Tia was standing on a root. She was in no danger of sinking because she'd planned the route carefully.

"Don't do this, Tia."

"I have to. It's what he wants me to do."

"He?"

Balancing on the root, Tia unbuttoned her blouse and pulled it down on her shoulders. Then she turned so that Carrie could see her back in the moonlight. The tattooed horns on her shoulders sent a terrible fear spiraling through Carrie.

She put a trembling hand to her mouth. *"No."*

"It was the only way I could get away from him," Tia whispered.

And so she'd become him.

The thing she feared most.

Someone came rushing out of the woods and stopped short at the edge of the bog. Carrie's heart leaped to her throat. She thought at first it was Nick....

Then a voice growled from the darkness, "What the hell are you doing? You said you just wanted to scare her."

"She is scared," Tia said. "Can't you tell?"

"You can't leave her here like this." The man came out of the shadows then, and Carrie recognized him. It was Pete Trawick. "I didn't sign on for murder."

"Well, then it's lucky that your job is finished." Tia's hand reached into her pocket and slowly drew out a weapon. "I took this from your friend, Nick," she said and fired.

Trawick pitched forward without a sound.

Calmly, Tia lowered the gun. "He wouldn't give me the time of day," she continued, as if she hadn't just shot a man in cold blood. "But naturally, he fell for you. They always do, don't they, Carrie? And you like to lead them on, too. That's how we ended up in that cabin," she said. "And that's why I am what I am."

Carrie had said nothing for several long minutes. She knew better than to show her fear. That's what *he* wanted....

The mud was past her knees now. It was all she could do not to struggle.

Tia moved out of the bog and sat down on a limb. "I think I'll just sit here and watch for a while. There's still plenty of time."

"You won't be able to get off the island," Carrie said. "The police will see you."

"So what? I'm an innocent victim, remember?"

"No, you're not. The police already suspect you killed Trey."

"I suppose you made sure of that." She got to her feet and dusted off her pants. "Don't worry about me, Carrie. I have a way off the island. And the police will never find me. I've been coming down here for years. It's the perfect place to disappear."

With one last look at Carrie, she turned and walked off into the darkness.

THE MUD WAS PAST her thighs now, and Carrie's panic had taken over. She strained toward the tree root to pull herself out, but the action only made her sink faster and deeper.

She screamed, but she knew there was no one around to hear her.

"I'm sorry, Nick," she whispered. "I'm sorry I got you involved in this...."

"Carrie!"

She must be hallucinating, Carrie thought,

because she could have sworn she heard him calling out to her.

"Carrie!"

It was him!

"I'm over here! I'm in the bog...."

He came out of the woods and stopped dead when he saw her. Carrie had never been so glad to see anyone in her life.

"I'm stuck," she whispered.

"Stop moving. Stay as still as you can."

The mud was up to her waist now. "I can't breathe...."

"I'll get you out. Just don't move, okay."

Lying on his stomach, Nick inched toward her until she could reach his hand. He grabbed her arm and started pulling.

It wasn't working. He couldn't get her free.

Behind Nick, Pete Trawick had staggered to his feet. He was bleeding profusely from the wound in his chest, but somehow he'd managed to draw his gun.

"Nick! Behind you!"

He whirled just as Trawick fired, and the

bullet buried itself in the mud where Nick had been lying moments before.

Trawick fired again, this time just missing Carrie, and Nick lunged toward him. He plowed into Trawick and the two men went crashing to the ground. Trawick was wounded and he must have been weakened from the loss of blood. But he was bigger than Nick and he was fighting for his life. The weapon was between them and they struggled for what seemed an eternity.

And all the while, Carrie continued to sink. The mud was up to her chest now. She could barely hold her arms up.

The gun went off and she screamed. For a split second, neither man moved, and then Nick disengaged himself from the dead man, and staggered to his feet.

Falling to the ground at the edge of the bog, he slid toward her again. When he grabbed her this time, Carrie could tell he would never let go. They would either both make it out...or sink together.

He pulled with what seemed like super-human strength, and finally Carrie could feel the mud give away. She had to fight the impulse to try and kick her way out. Instead, she remained perfectly still and let Nick do all the work.

When he had her free, he wrapped his arms around her and held on tight.

Carrie clung to him. "It was Tia," she whispered. "She left me here."

She felt him stiffen. "I was afraid of something like that."

She drew back and stared up at him. "You knew?"

"I was starting to have some suspicions," he said.

"Why didn't you say anything?"

"Because I knew you wouldn't believe me."

"Trey—"

Nick's arms tightened around her. "Don't even say it. This isn't your fault, Carrie."

"But she became *him*." She squeezed

her eyes closed. "What'll happen to her now?"

"The police will pick her up. She'll have to undergo extensive psychiatric evaluation, and eventually stand trial for Hollinger's murder."

"What if the police never find her. She said she's been coming here for years. She has a boat—"

"I wouldn't worry about that. I found her boat days ago, and I told the cops about it last night. They may have already picked her up."

"I don't think I can face her again. Not yet."

"Just take it one step at a time," Nick said as he pulled her to her feet. "That's all you can do."

"You saved my life," she whispered. "If you hadn't found me, I would have just disappeared. But you came looking for me."

"And lucky for us both, I found you." He bent his head and kissed her.

THE NEXT DAY, CARRIE stood on the pier and waited for the boat that would take her back to the mainland. Tia had been apprehended the night before and taken into custody. Carrie and Nick had both given their statements and now there was nothing more to do but say goodbye.

She could hear the sound of an engine in the distance and she turned to Nick. "The boat's coming. I guess this is it then."

He nodded. "It's all over, Carrie. You'll be fine now. You're a pretty amazing woman. You know that, don't you?"

Her heart thudded at the way he looked down at her. "I'm not special."

"Yes, you are. You're a survivor. That's how I know you'll get through this."

She swallowed past a sudden lump in her throat. "What are you going to do now?"

"Go back to headquarters," he said with a shrug. "Not much left to do here."

"Sorry about your assignment."

He smiled. "There'll be other assignments. What about you?"

"I'm going home, going back to work. It's time to get on with my life. I'm tired of living in the past."

"This may not be the best time to ask you this," Nick said slowly. "But could I call you sometime?" He sounded endearingly unsure of himself. "We could have dinner or catch a movie…."

"You mean date?" Carrie asked in surprise.

He shrugged. "Sure, why not? Key West is only a two-hour drive from Miami. Less by air, and I get up there pretty often…." He trailed off. "Things got pretty intense pretty fast here on the island. Back in the real world, you may decide you don't want any reminders of what happened. If you change your mind—"

"I won't." She fished in her bag for a pen. Turning his hand over, she scribbled her home and cell phone numbers on his palm. "So you won't lose it," she whispered.

He lifted his hand and touched her hair. "I'm going to miss you."

"I'll miss you, too."

They both fell silent then as they watched the boat slowly approach the island. Nick helped her in, and as the driver turned and headed back toward the mainland, she turned to wave.

Nick didn't return her wave, but he watched her until the boat was out of sight.

* * * * *

CAPE DIABLO *continues next month*
with UNDENIABLE PROOF
by B. J. Daniels.
Available August 2006
wherever Harlequin Books are sold.

HARLEQUIN ROMANCE®

The rush of falling in love,

Cosmopolitan,
international settings,

Believable, feel-good stories
about today's women

The compelling thrill
of romantic excitement

It could happen to you!

EXPERIENCE
HARLEQUIN ROMANCE!

Available wherever Harlequin Books are sold.

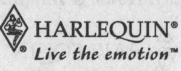

HARLEQUIN®
Live the emotion™

www.eHarlequin.com

HROMDIR04

HARLEQUIN®

AMERICAN *Romance*®

Invites *you* to experience lively, heartwarming all-American romances

Every month, we bring you four strong, sexy men, and four women who know what they want—and go all out to get it.

Enjoy stories about the pursuit of love, family and marriage in America today— *everywhere* people live and love!

AMERICAN *Romance*—
Heart, Home & Happiness

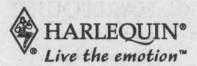 HARLEQUIN®
Live the emotion™

www.eHarlequin.com   HARDIR104

HARLEQUIN®
INTRIGUE®
WE'LL LEAVE YOU BREATHLESS!

If you've been looking for thrilling tales of
contemporary passion and sensuous love stories
with taut, edge-of-the-seat suspense—then
you'll love Harlequin Intrigue!

Every month, you'll meet six new heroes
who are guaranteed to make your spine tingle
and your pulse pound. With them you'll enter
into the exciting world of Harlequin Intrigue—
where your life is on the line
and so is your heart!

THAT'S INTRIGUE—
ROMANTIC SUSPENSE
AT ITS BEST!

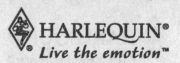

HARLEQUIN®
Live the emotion™

www.eHarlequin.com   INTDIR104

...there's more to the story!

Superromance.
A *big* satisfying read about unforgettable
characters. Each month we offer *six* very different
stories that range from family drama to adventure
and mystery, from highly emotional stories to
romantic comedies—and much more! Stories
about people you'll believe in and care about.
Stories too compelling to put down....

Our authors are among today's *best* romance
writers. You'll find familiar names and talented
newcomers. Many of them are award winners—
and you'll see why!

If you want the biggest and best
in romance fiction, you'll get it
from Superromance!

Emotional, Exciting, Unexpected...

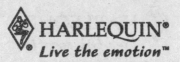

www.eHarlequin.com   HSDIR104

HARLEQUIN®
Presents

The world's bestselling romance series...
The series that brings you your favorite authors,
month after month:

Helen Bianchin...Emma Darcy
Lynne Graham...Penny Jordan
Miranda Lee...Sandra Marton
Anne Mather...Carole Mortimer
Susan Napier...Michelle Reid

and many more uniquely talented authors!

Wealthy, powerful, gorgeous men...
Women who have feelings just like your own...
The stories you love, set in exotic, glamorous locations...

HARLEQUIN®
Presents

Seduction and Passion Guaranteed!

www.eHarlequin.com

HPDIR104

Harlequin Historicals®
Historical Romantic Adventure!

From rugged lawmen and
valiant knights to defiant heiresses
and spirited frontierswomen,
Harlequin Historicals will
capture your imagination with
their dramatic scope, passion
and adventure.

Harlequin Historicals . . .
they're too good to miss!